Longarm compressed his lips grimly, a scalding ache in his throat as he contemplated the Kid's ruined body.

"Get them for me, Jed."

"I will, Kid. That's a promise."

"They . . . laughed . . . while . . . did this to me."

"Even Consuela?"

"She was . . . worse. She . . ."

He began to cough and was not able to finish. Longarm went for more water, but when he returned to the cot, the Kid was dead—a merciful release.

Longarm looked down at the Kid. Badge or no badge, Bat Coulter's gang would pay for this.

TABOR EVANS

LONGARM

AND THE
ROCKY MOUNTAIN CHASE

J

JOVE BOOKS, NEW YORK

LONGARM AND THE ROCKY MOUNTAIN CHASE

A Jove Book / published by arrangement with
the author

PRINTING HISTORY
Jove edition / July 1987

ISBN: 0-515-09056-5

Jove Books are published by the Berkley Publishing Group,
200 Madison Avenue, New York, NY 10016.
The name "Jove" and the "J" logo
are trademarks belonging to Jove Publications, Inc.

PRINTED IN THE UNITED STATES OF AMERICA

10 9 8 7 6 5 4 3 2 1

Chapter 1

Longarm had heard the expression "out of the blue" before. Now he knew what it meant. He pulled his horse
to a sudden halt and glanced swiftly around him. It was
late afternoon and he was riding along the crest of a
ridge above a stand of aspen on the western slope of the
Divide. A moment before, the air had gone eerily still.
Now the hairs on the back of his neck and along his
arms were beginning to tingle. Then he saw quite a few
of the hairs in his mount's mane begin to straighten up.
At once he knew he was in trouble.

Dry lightning.

Before he could take cover, a lightning bolt seared
out of the sky and took out a tree less than ten yards
from him. Another bolt slammed to earth even closer,
slicing a boulder neatly in two. The stench of Hades
was too much for Longarm's mount. Terrified, the poor
beast reared almost straight up, pawing the charged air

1

with flailing hoofs, then toppled back. Longarm slammed heavily to the ground under him. Before Longarm could untangle his left leg from the stirrup, the horse galloped off, dragging Longarm after him.

His shoulders and head took a fearful pounding as the spooked beast, keeping just ahead of the lightning bolts that continued to sear the high, thin atmosphere all about the ridge, went straight for the lip of a gorge. Almost, but not quite in time, Longarm twisted his leg free of the stirrup just as the deranged horse charged off into space.

Longarm's momentum carried him over the edge also. He felt the gravel rolling under his back as he bumped down the steep slope. Reaching out frantically, he managed to grab the roots of a gnarled juniper and hang on. It stopped his plunge, but before he could find another handhold, the juniper's roots pulled free of the light soil, and Longarm continued his plunge, sliding untidily backward down the slope. For an instant he was airborne. A patch of sky arched across his line of vision before he came to an abrupt, slamming halt against a projecting ledge, the back of his head snapping back hard against it.

Adding insult to injury, the sky now opened up, and he was lashed by a downpour so heavy he was in danger of being flushed off the ledge. Funneled torrents of water sluiced down upon the ledge and past him into the gorge below. As suddenly as it had begun, the rain squall ceased. A bright sky appeared above him. He pulled himself painfully to his feet, but the muddy ledge was dangerously slippery. Pebbles flew out from under his boots as he lurched backward and slammed back down again onto the ledge.

2

He lay on his back, his senses reeling, drifting off finally while the sun baked him dry. What pulled him back to consciousness was the end of a rope tickling his forehead. He opened his eyes. Someone above him on the ridge had snaked a rope down to him. He couldn't make out the face. It was shaded by a hatbrim and, besides, the distance was too great.

"Grab it!" came the shout from above. It was a woman's voice, husky, commanding.

He found that his left hand was no help at all as he reached up to grab the rope. It grew taut in the grasp of his right hand and, as he clung to it, he was slowly pulled upright. Earlier, he had felt little pain in his left side—only a tingling numbness. Now, however, the discomfort was intense enough for him to glance down to see how bad it was. All he saw was raw, scraped flesh with no broken bones sticking out. His trouser leg had been torn almost to shreds and his frock coat hung on his back in strips, with only his vest still a service-able garment. His derringer sat in its fob pocket, and his cross-draw rig had remained intact, his .44 double-action Colt still resting in its holster.

"Hold it!" he called. "Let up on the rope!"

The rope slackened and he looped it twice around his waist.

"Okay!"

Again the rope grew taut and began to pull him up the side of the ravine. The woman remained in sight; he could see her guiding the rope back to whoever was pulling on it. With only his right leg and hand capable of helping, he did what he could to keep himself from slamming into the boulders and rock strata that jutted out from the cliff's face. When he reached the gorge's

3

rim, the woman grabbed his right hand and hauled him up beside her.

Longarm saw that she was alone. She had secured the rope to her saddle horn with a half-hitch and it was her horse, backing up slowly, which had been hauling him up the rock face.

"You all right?" she asked.

"A little banged up, I reckon," he replied, "but the hinges are still in place and most of the bolts've held."

"I saw what happened from that ridge over there," she said, pointing to a dim line of trees, a deep ravine intervening between it and where they now stood. "Sorry it took so long for me to get here."

"No need to apologize," he said woozily, wishing he could manufacture a chair to sit down on. "You did get here, and I would've had a dim time of climbing up that rock face all by myself."

She smiled and he found himself smiling back.

The woman was in her thirties, full-bodied and handsome. Her eyes were a lustrous brown, set wide apart above a strong, slender nose. Her lower lip was full, passionate, her jaw square, the tiniest hint of a dimple in its center. Her thick mass of auburn hair was caught behind her head with a leather thong and allowed to extend down her back. She was a woman in her prime. Her hips, encased in Levi's, flared opulently and her upthrust bosom pressed urgently against the pull of the blue men's cotton shirt she wore.

If Longarm had been a kid again, he would have puckered his lips and whistled a salute to her lush, ripe beauty. And at the moment he felt giddy enough to do just that. But before he could utter a sound, he felt his senses begin to reel. He reached out to her for support, then toppled to the ground. He remembered her concern as she tried to help him back up onto his feet. Then he passed out.

He awoke on a cot in a large room. He was aware of a man's eyes studying him coldly. He turned his head. The man watching him was in the middle of the room, sitting with his arms folded onto a deal table. His gun-belt was slung over the back of his chair, and a nearly empty bottle of whiskey sat on the table in front of him. When he saw Longarm turn his head to face him, he tipped the bottle up and drank deeply. His undershirt was filthy, his dusty vest torn. He might have been handsome once, but now, pushing forty, his p le, narrow face had a surly cast to it. His gray, close-set eyes were shifty, his chin slack. He looked as soft as bread dough and as treacherous as a scorpion.

Filling the far wall behind the man at the table was a fieldstone fireplace. At the foot of Longarm's cot a doorway led into the kitchen. The smell of hot coffee and the aroma of baking bread wafted through it. Longarm could hear the busy clatter of a woman at the stove.

Longarm tried to sit up, groaned, and lay back down. He was sore all over. There wasn't a muscle or a bone that didn't ache.

The fellow at the table shucked his broad-brimmed hat back off his forehead and got to his feet.

"Serena! He's come around," the man called.

A second later, wiping her hands on her apron, the woman who had hauled Longarm off the ledge appeared in the kitchen doorway. When she saw Longarm was awake, she smiled warmly at him.

"How do you feel?" she asked.

"Like I been run over by a train."

"I can imagine. That was some fall you took." Then, referring to his own comments earlier, "But as you say, all the hinges are still in place, and as far as I can tell, you have no broken bones."

"That ain't the way it feels."

"All right, mister," said the man at the table. "Just who in hell are you? What's your business in these parts?" As he spoke, he got up and strode toward Longarm. His surly hostility angered the lawman, but Longarm kept his temper and forced a smile.

"I'm just passin' through," he replied. "I hope I haven't caused you and your missus any trouble. You both have my gratitude for your hospitality."

"Hell, mister," said the man, "your gratitude ain't worth a pitcher of warm spit if you don't tell me what you're doin' messing around this high country. You don't look like no prospector."

"I told you. I'm just ridin' through."

"And you expect me to believe that, do you?"

"Frankly," Longarm said, his voice no longer conciliatory, "I don't care what you believe."

Longarm glanced at Serena. It was startling that a woman of her quality could be married to such a lout. He could see from the look on her face that she understood precisely what he was thinking.

"You must not mind Lester," she told him. "He just stopped by on his way back to someplace else. Soon's he finishes that whiskey he brought with him." She turned on Lester then, her look cold enough to put out a fire. "Isn't that right, Lester?"

"Nope, it ain't, Serena. I done come back to stay."

Her face paled. "You can't mean that, Lester."

"Sure I can. You can't kick me out. I got rights. I'm your husband."

"In name only. We're through, Lester."

"No we ain't—not unless I say we are. And I think maybe I'll keep my claim on you."

"You've been talking to Bat Coulter."

Lester grinned. "He's a good friend, and that's a fact."

"This ranch is mine. And this house, too. And I want you out of it. If I have to, I'll go to the sheriff."

"You think the sheriff will help you kick a man out of his own home? This is a family matter. We're husband and wife. A sheriff ain't got no jurisdiction in a man's castle."

Furious, Serena glanced at Longarm. "I'm sorry," she told him. "It's not fittin' you should be hearin' this." Then she looked back at Lester. "We'll finish this discussion outside."

She marched past Lester, opened the door, and stepped outside. Swaggering, Lester followed her. Longarm flung aside the single sheet that covered him and sat up. He ignored his creaking limbs and pushed himself upright. Grimacing slightly, he reached back for the bedsheet and wrapped it around his naked figure, then went to the doorway.

Serena was standing only a few feet away, Lester's face pressed close to hers. He was shouting at her. Abruptly, Serena slapped him. Lester was game. He slapped her back, first on one cheek, then on the other. Serena's knees sagged. She would have gone down if she hadn't reached out and grabbed a fence post.

An old, stove-up cowpoke in a floppy-brimmed hat hurried out of the bunkhouse toward them. A ragged-

7

looking sheepdog limped after him. The old man looked
at least fifty, maybe older. His parchment-like cheeks
were covered with a faint white stubble. He had obviously seen Lester strike his wife. There was fire in his
eyes as he approached the two, but Longarm knew he
would be no match for Lester.

Serena turned at his approach. "No, Abe!" she told
him. "This is between me and Lester."

"I can whip that polecat!" he insisted. "Let me at
him, Serena."

"No! Please, Abe. Do as I say!"

Abe pulled up, confused. "I just saw him," he said,
his thin voice trembling with outrage. "He hit you!"

"Please, Abe. Just go back to the bunkhouse."

"That's right, old man," Lester told him. "Go back
into your hole or I'll piss all over you."

Abe glared at Lester for a long moment, then turned
and went back to the bunkhouse, his dog trailing after
him. As soon as he disappeared inside, Lester grabbed
Serena and pulled her roughly toward him.

"You said the right thing, Serena," Lester told her,
chuckling. "This *is* between us. Just you and me. And
I'm your lord and master! Time you learned that."

He yanked her closer and tried to kiss her. Frantically, Serena tried to twist out of his grasp. Laughing,
Lester managed to plant a clumsy kiss on her cheek,
then tried to catch her lips with his. In desperation, she
pounded on his chest. Giving up suddenly, Lester
stepped back and punched her solidly in the gut.

As she knifed over, he caught her. "Now maybe
you'll listen to reason," he told her. His arms slid down
her waist and he pulled her hard against him.

Longarm had seen enough. He left the cabin and

headed toward them. He felt just a little silly dressed like a Roman senator in his makeshift toga, but there was no help for it. Lester was mauling the woman who had saved his life.

Lester saw Longarm coming. He pushed Serena away and swung around to face him. "Well, now. Look who's comin' to save the lady in distress!"

Longarm said nothing. He just kept coming.

"Please, mister," Serena said. "I'll handle this."

"You ain't doing so well," Longarm told her.

"You gonna do any better?" Lester asked.

Bending swiftly, Lester reached back behind his boot and straightened up with a long skinning knife in his hand. Longarm whipped off his bedsheet and threw it over Lester's head and shoulders. As Lester struggled to fight free of the sheet, Longarm stepped in close, clasped both hands together, and brought them down on the man's wildly bobbing head. Lester sagged forward. Longarm swung his knee up and caught Lester in the chest. Lester grunted and staggered back awkwardly, his knife ripping through the sheet. Grabbing Lester's wrist, Longarm twisted the knife from the man's grasp, then flung him to the ground. As Lester struck it, Longarm flung the bedsheet aside and kicked Lester in the face. Lester's nose became a bloody smear. He rolled over, then rocked dazedly on his hands and knees, the hole in his face dripping like a faucet as he blinked blearily at Longarm.

Longarm knelt beside Lester and held the tip of the knife to Lester's Adam's apple, using just enough pressure to draw blood.

"First of all," Longarm told Lester, "I want you apologize to Serena."

9

When Lester hesitated, Longarm increased the knife's pressure. A thin trickle of blood moved down his neck and under his grimy shirt collar. Lester blinked unhappily up at Serena.

"Sorry," he burbled through the blood seeping into his mouth.

"No," said Longarm. "Say, 'I'm sorry, Serena.'"

"I'm . . . sorry, Serena."

"That's better. Now tell her you'll be moving on— that you won't be bothering her any more."

Lester hesitated. Longarm pressed the blade in deeper. More blood oozed out around the knife point. Lester looked up at his wife. "I won't bother you no more. I'm movin' on."

"That's fine," said Longarm.

He stood up, aware for the first time that without the bedsheet, he was standing naked before Serena. He snatched up the bedsheet, then looked at Lester. "Get on your horse."

Lester got to his feet. For a fleeting moment defiance flickered in his eyes. But it faded swiftly enough. Holding a filthy bandanna against his ruined nose, Lester turned and scurried toward the barn.

The bedsheet still wrapped around him, Longarm headed back to the cabin with Serena. A moment later, a loaded rifle in her hand, she stood in the cabin doorway with Longarm as Lester rode up to the cabin for his sidearm. She flung his gun and gunbelt up to him. He caught it and strapped it around his waist, his smeared nose giving him a grotesque aspect.

"I won't forget this, mister," he said, his eyes boring bleakly into Longarm's.

"You better not."

Lester pulled his horse around and rode out of the compound.

"You got any idea where he's heading?" Longarm asked, watching him go.

"Back to Bat Coulter and the rest of his bunch of misfits. They've got a hideout somewhere in the mountains, last I heard."

She turned then to face him.

"Now, just who the devil are you, mister?"

Longarm's present mission prompted him not to give his real name. "I'm Jed Morgan, Serena."

"Was Lester right? Are you just a drifter?"

"Is that what *you* think?"

"Not after the way you just handled Lester."

For a moment his eyes held hers. Then she looked away, blushing. The delicious aroma of baking bread drifted out of the kitchen toward him. "Something smells good," he told her.

"Oh!" she cried, spinning about and running for the kitchen, the rifle still in her hand. "The bread!"

Longarm slowly, carefully walked back to the cot and lay down on it. His recent exertions had left him surprisingly weak and enormously hungry. But at least he knew for sure now that his fall onto that ledge had not seriously crippled him. Nevertheless, he was now suddenly very tired. He closed his eyes and drifted off into a deep sleep.

It was early morning of a new day. A rooster was crowing. He blinked at the light flooding through the window over his cot. He turned his head. Serena was sitting in a chair beside his cot, a bowl of hot broth in one hand, a wooden spoon in the other. Abe was standing

11

behind her. When he caught Longarm's eyes, he smiled quickly, happily.

Serena smiled. "This here's Abe, Jed," she said. "He figured the smell of this broth would wake you up."

"Howdy, Abe," Longarm said. "Pleased to meet you."

"And I'm right proud to meet the man punched that turd Lester into next week."

"Didn't like him, huh?"

"There's a special place in hell for his kind."

Longarm sat up, keeping the bedsheet around him as he rested his feet on the floor. He was ravenous. Serena pressed the wooden spoon to his lips. The broth was delicious. It had pieces of turnip and succulent chunks of mutton in it. Warmth spread throughout his long frame, invigorating him. In a short while he had finished off the broth and was on his second cup of coffee, looking forward to a third.

At the table he joined Serena and Abe for his third cup.

"You've got a problem," she said, glancing mischievously at the torn bedsheet clinging to his figure.

"I need duds."

"Less'n you want to go around looking like a haunt," Abe grinned.

"How tall are you?" Serena asked.

"A little more'n six feet."

She appraised him approvingly. "And you have about the right build, I should say."

"What've you got in mind?"

"My husband's clothing."

"Lester's?"

"No, my first husband. Jason Brockway. A fine gen-

12

tleman and a lover of horseflesh. This horse ranch was his idea, and for a while the three of us were quite successful. Then Jason died of Mountain Fever."

"I am sorry."

"Not as much as I am."

"He was a right fine gentleman," said Abe.

"How'd you come to hitch up with Lester?" Longarm asked her.

"I married Lester for all the wrong reasons. But don't blame Abe. He tried to warn me. Anyway, God has punished me for my foolishness. Lester was the foreman of the ranch, and when Jason died, he was very attentive. I knew little or nothing about him, but that did not seem to matter at the time." She shuddered. "It was a terrible mistake."

"A snake in the grass," Abe said. "All smiles and concern, until he got his hands on Serena."

"You mean he took advantage of you while you were not thinking clearly," Longarm suggested.

"And I let him."

"Anyway, do you think your first husband's clothes will fit?"

"We'll just have to see." She turned to Abe. "What do you think?"

"Mebbe," he said. "Jed here is a mite taller, I'd say. And he's got quite a pair of shoulders."

"His clothes are in the steamer truck. I'll get them."

"What about my coat and pants?" Longarm asked.

"They were ripped to shreds. I threw them out."

Longarm frowned. In his coat's inside pocket he kept his wallet, containing his marshal's shield, not to mention the folding money he carried as well. "My wallet was in the jacket's inside pocket," he told her.

13

"There was a long rent down the left side. The lining and everything were ripped out. I am afraid your wallet is probably somewhere at the bottom of that gorge. How much did you lose? I'd be glad to advance you whatever you might need."

"What about my vest?"

"Oh, that was intact," she said, amused, "and with it your watch and that cute little gun."

"It's a derringer, Serena. In close quarters it can pack a deadly wallop."

Abe tipped his head and appraised him coolly. "You're a gambler, am I right?"

"What makes you think that?"

"I heard gamblers kept little guns like yours hidden on them in case someone questioned the deal."

"Did you, now?"

"Well, are you a gambler?"

"You know what they say, Serena. Life's a gamble."

She sighed, finished her coffee and stood up. As she disappeared into the kitchen, she said, "It's gamble, all right. And you men have all the cards. I'll get out that trunk as soon as I can."

"I'll need a bath first," he called after her.

She stepped back out of the kitchen and looked at him. "All right," she said. "I'll heat some water for you."

Longarm thought he caught a hint of mischief in her dark eyes, but he could not be sure.

He *was* sure not long after as she knelt beside the huge wooden washtub and reached for the long-handled brush he was wielding.

"Here," she said, taking it from him. "Let me."

He did not argue as she began laving his back with

14

the soaped brush, her strokes gentle yet firm. When she finished, she pushed him back and began stroking his chest. He closed his eyes and let the long strokes lull him. Her presence was intoxicating. He could smell her hair and the sweetness of her breath. Closer and closer she leaned as she laved his chest and thighs, and he found himself noticing the outline of her two nipples as they thrust against her damp, clinging blouse.

When she put aside the brush, soaped a washcloth and began reaching down into his crotch, he forced himself to look away. But before long his manhood betrayed him. He heard Serena catch her breath, then her soft, delighted laughter. He turned his head slightly and caught her teasing eyes with his. Her hand was still in the water. Abruptly it closed about his erection. He pulled her close and kissed her, aware of the steam coiling up about them. She returned his kiss with a savage need that startled him.

Without a word he stood, lifted her in his dripping arms, and carried her out of the kitchen into her bedroom.

"We'll get the bedsheets all wet," she protested weakly.

"It doesn't matter," he told her, letting her gently down onto her bed.

Undressing her was no problem. Under her wide skirt she wore nothing, nor was she wearing any corset. She yanked her blouse over her head and tossed it aside, and they were both as God had made them as he moved swiftly to cover her, then thrust gently, entering her warm, eager sheath. Gasping softly, she swung her legs up and crossed them behind his buttocks, then flung both arms around his shoulders and hugged him to her.

He bent and kissed her, rocking gently back and forth. Her mouth opened in a gasp and soon she was thrusting urgently under him, while he slammed deeper and deeper into her. Climaxing, she cried out, flinging her head back while he closed his mouth about her shoulder in a gentle bite and hung on as he, too, climaxed.

He rolled off her, cupping one breast in his big hand and kneading it gently. She placed her hand over his hand and lay on her back, gazing up at the ceiling, her breathing still heavy. For a long, delicious moment they lay like that, saying nothing, drinking in each other's nearness. Then he turned his head and kissed her lightly on the cheek. She smiled and looked at him almost tenderly. Their lovemaking had ben astonishingly swift—taking place in a kind of feverish dream—and now came the sharp clarity.

"My God, what must you think of me?" she whispered.

"You don't need to talk like that."

"But . . . but I hardly know you."

"And I hardly know you, but I feel no shame." He reached over and brushed a lock of damp hair off her forehead. "Only gratitude—and a sweet emptiness."

She sighed and closed her eyes in relief. "You understand, don't you? Oh, I knew you would. It was that week of caring for you, gazing on your long, battered body. Some nights I caught sight of . . . that part of you coming alive. It meant to me you were getting well. But . . . it was most exciting. I tried not to think of it."

"Stop explaining."

"But . . . who are you? A gambler, a drifter?"

"I'm the man whose life you saved. And I just want to thank you."

16

She gazed at him with her dark, deep eyes for a long, long moment. "All right," she said huskily, "thank me. Now!"

Longarm rolled over onto his elbows, leaned over her and kissed first one nipple, then the other. She dropped her arms about his neck and pressed him close to her, sighing. Closing his lips about one nipple, he worked it gently for a long while, aware of it lifting sharply under his lips, becoming as hard as a bullet. She began to heave gently under him. His lips released her nipple and moved slowly down her rounded belly, pausing at her navel. She moaned softly and stirred languorously under him. He became aware of the fruity, intoxicating scent of her as his lips continued on into the sharp hollow inside her flaring hips.

Reaching down, Serena's fingers found his shock of heavy hair as she groaned, lifting herself to him. . . .

Chapter 2

They were dozing in each other's arms when Abe's frantic pounding on the cabin door aroused them. Serena jumped up, slipped into her blouse and skirt, and hurried from the bedroom.

Sitting up, Longarm flung a blanket over his naked frame and listened intently as Serena opened the door.

"Riders!" Abe cried. "Five in all."

"Who's leading them? Lester?"

"No, Bat Coulter!"

"Get back to the bunkhouse and stay there!"

"But, Serena—!"

"You heard me. You know what those men are like! They're killers!"

Longarm heard the door slam. He swung off the bed as Serena appeared in the bedroom doorway.

"You heard?"

"Yep."

She looked at his gaunt nakedness with a sudden, rueful smile. "You'll need clothes."

"And a gun."

"That derringer?"

"That too, but it doesn't have much range. What about my Colt?"

"I'll get it."

She disappeared and returned a moment later with an armful of her husband's duds and Longarm's cross-draw rig and Colt. There was no underwear and the pants did not fit as snugly as his own had, but they would do. The frock coat was cut from brown tweed, expensively tailored, and there was barely enough room in the shoulders. All in all, a good enough fit, seeing the clothes had been made for a dead man. Serena brought clean socks and his own low-heeled army boots. In a moment he was on his feet, buckling on his cross-draw rig and checking out the Colt. That finished, he glanced up at Serena. "I need a hat. My own is still at the bottom of that gorge."

She left and returned a moment later with her first husband's black Stetson. It was nearly new and had a low, flat crown, with a brim somewhat wider than Longarm's own hat. Glancing in the mirror over her dresser, he adjusted the brim carefully. The brim was so wide, it kept his forehead and eyes in darkness, leaving only his jaw and the flaring uptwist of his longhorn mustache clearly visible. At first glance, even Marshal Billy Vail would have had trouble recognizing him.

In that instant, Longarm made his decision.

"You better get to the door," he told Serena. "I'll keep back out of sight until you need me."

20

As she left the bedroom, Longarm followed her and took a post alongside the window nearest the door. Keeping out of sight, he peered through a small hole in the shade.

The lead rider, Bat Coulter, was forking a small but heavily muscled pinto that walked with a slightly splay-footed stride. Coulter himself was dressed pretty flashily. He was wearing a dark brown shirt, and at his neck he had knotted a deep-purple cravat joined to the collar by a silver ring and fastened to the shirt with a pearl-studded stickpin. His buckskin trousers were a dark, chocolate brown, flaring at the knee and ending just below the tops of soft, soot-black boots. His unbuttoned burgundy-colored vest could be seen dimly behind the long black duster he wore like a cloak, sleeves empty. His flat-topped wide-brimmed hat was black, its hue softened by a gray pall of trail dust.

As Coulter rode closer, Longarm got a clearer vision of the gang leader's face. He sported a full, handlebar mustache, silken black whiskers of medium length, and a heavy fall of hair reaching clear to his shoulders. His nose was a hooked beak, his dark eyes fierce and uncompromising as they peered out from under thick brows. He carried himself with an air of indomitable purpose, and the four riders flanking him seemed just as purposeful.

Longarm smiled. He had already memorized Bat Coulter's description, for the man Serena and Lester knew as Bat Coulter was in reality Bart Cotten, a gun-slick only two years out of Yuma and now the leader of the toughest gang west of Denver. They had robbed three trains in the past two years, and during the most recent heist a postal worker had been gunned down, which gave Marshal Billy Vail an urgent incentive to bring Coulter and his gang to heel.

Two weeks earlier rumor reached Denver that Coulter was due to make another strike, this time upon the Denver Western line hauling gold dust between Denver and the Link Mine near Red Cliff. At once Billy Vail sent Longarm out to join forces with the Red Cliff sheriff, Glenn Scott, to help him comb the area in search of Coulter's gang. It was high, rocky, difficult country, most of it vertical—but Longarm was familiar with it from earlier assignments, and it was hoped that his knowledge of the terrain would help the sheriff and his posse to ferret out the gang's hideout. But, as luck would have it, here was the Coulter gang, and Longarm had not yet reached Red Cliff.

The man who now called himself Bat Coulter halted his pinto in front of the cabin door, his riders milling about him. Serena opened the door and stepped out. She was carrying a double-barreled Greener.

At sight of the shotgun, Coulter doffed his cap and smiled. It was not a pleasant smile. "Howdy, Mrs. Gullick."

"State your business, Coulter."

"It's your husband we want—Lester. Is he about?"

"I sent him packing, and in the future, Coulter, I'd appreciate it if you would not refer to that polecat as my husband."

"I'll remember that." Coulter smiled and looked quickly, sharply about him, then back down at Serena. "He lit out, you say?"

"Yes."

"That's real strange. I was expecting him to meet me here. We got some business, important business. He better not be weaselin' out on us. You sure you ain't hidin' him from me?"

"That's the last thing I'd do, Coulter—hide that worm from you and your killers."

"Now, now," Coulter grinned, holding up his hand as if to ward off her anger. "No sense in getting all riled if you're tellin' the truth."

"I am, damn you!"

A redheaded fellow with a narrow, pocked face nudged his horse up alongside Coulter's and whispered something to him. Smiling, Coulter withdrew his six-gun. Without seeming to aim, he punched a shot in Longarm's direction. The round shattered the window beside Longarm and ripped through the shade. Longarm let it snap up to reveal him standing by the window. It was foolish for him to try to keep out of sight now. He left the window, walked out of the cabin, and took a stand beside Serena.

"Sorry, mister," drawled Coulter. "Thought you was someone else hidin' behind this filly's skirts."

The redhead leaned forward in his stirrups and peered closely at Longarm. "What's your name, mister?" he demanded.

"Smith. John Smith."

Coulter grinned. "Well, now, for a man on the run, that's sure enough a familiar name. You got a posse on your tail, Mr. Smith?"

"That's for me to know and you to find out."

Coulter thumb-cocked his revolver and pointed it casually at Longarm's forehead. "I think I'm going to find out right now."

Longarm shrugged. "Now that I think of it, there just might be a dodger or two out on me."

23

"Your real name, then. I want it."

"Morgan. Jed Morgan."

Coulter frowned. "No outlaws around that I know of with that name. You sure you're wanted?"

"I'm wanted."

"What for?"

"I raised a stage outside Nevada City a couple of years ago. My horse went lame or I would've been a rich man."

Coulter chuckled appreciatively and holstered his weapon. "Hell, that's ancient history, Morgan. You been forgotten by now."

Longarm shrugged.

"You lookin' for employment?"

Longarm shrugged. "Could be."

"Get a horse, then." Looking away from Longarm, Coulter addressed Serena. "If you see Les, you tell him he better join us at Hangman's Ridge before next Friday. You got that?"

"I told you," said Serena. "I sent him packin'."

"Aw, hell, Serena! You think he'll let go of you that easy? Once he gets his belly full of whiskey, he'll be back. Now you tell him what I just said. Hangman's Ridge."

"I'll tell him nothing. And if he does come back, I'll fill his whiskey belly full of buckshot."

Coulter laughed, pleased. "I believe you would, at that."

Serena said nothing more as she stepped back into the cabin doorway.

Coulter glanced back at Longarm. "We'll be movin' out now, Morgan," Coulter said, wheeling his horse. "Catch up—soon's you say goodbye to Les's wife!"

There was a sharp bark of ribald laughter from the rest of the riders. Coulter spurred his pinto to the head of the gang and led them at a sudden fast gallop out of the compound. He wasn't giving Longarm all that much time to say goodbye to Serena. He turned to face her. She was staring at him in some consternation, her face pale.

"You mean you're really going to join Coulter's gang?" she asked. "I can't believe it."

"Things aren't always what they seem, Serena."

"What do you mean by that?"

"Believe half of what you see and nothing of what you hear. Meanwhile, keep an eye out for Lester. You and Abe. And don't be afraid to use that shotgun if he gives you any trouble."

"I won't."

"Good. Now, do you have a horse you can let me have?"

She thought a moment, then nodded. "A blood bay. He's big enough for you."

A few moments later, as he mounted up, Abe came out of the bunkhouse cradling a shotgun. He kept just in front of the bunkhouse and watched carefully while Serena reached up to take Longarm's hand.

"You're not an outlaw," she said. "You lied to Coulter."

Longarm made no effort to deny it.

"You're a lawman, ain't you?"

"I don't want to get you involved, Serena. The less you know about me, the better. As far as you or Abe know, I'm Jed Morgan."

She smiled, relieved. Then she released his hand and stepped back. "All right, then. Take care of yourself,

Jed Morgan. You're still pretty banged up."

"I'll be back."

"I hope so. Anyway, I'll be lookin' for you."

With a wave to Serena and Abe, Longarm pulled his bay around and rode after Bat Coulter. For her own sake, Longarm hoped he hadn't told Serena more than he should have.

What Coulter called Hangman's Ridge was not visible from the valley floor below. In order to reach it, the gang followed a narrow game trail through a heavily timbered hogback until they came to a huge boulder sitting hard against a sheer wall of rock. Close alongside the boulder, obscured by a thick undergrowth of vines and brush, a narrow defile led through the mountain to a hidden clearing beyond. At the far end of the clearing, perched on Hangman's Ridge, sat a log cabin, corrals, and barns. So narrow was the passage leading through the mountain to this hidden outpost that only one horse and rider could slip through at a time.

As Longarm emerged from the damp, treacherous passage and gazed ahead of him across the meadow to Coulter's cabin and outbuildings, he realized why finding this gang had been so difficult. No matter how long or how diligently he and Sheriff Scott combed this wild country, they could never have found this hideout unaided.

Riding across the meadow slightly behind the other gang members, Longarm had his first real chance to take them all in since he had caught up with them the day before. The rider who seemed closest to Coulter was Larson, the redhead. He was a slouching, angry man who seldom talked to anyone but Coulter. When-

26

ever he spoke to a fellow gang member, it came out usually as a rasping snarl. He could not even ask for the coffee pot without raising hackles. The rest of the gang members hated him cordially, but offered him grudging respect all the same. Aware of their feelings, Larson appeared to relish, even feed on them. Slight of build, he was as strong as cable wire. His eyes were green and shifty, his pockmarked face sallow. Whenever he sweated profusely, a strange, urine-like smell came from him. The other gang members took notice of this with winks and furtive smirks, but dared not mention it aloud for fear of being overheard and arousing Larson's wrath.

The gang member most at the mercy of Larson was the Kid, a youngster who did not look quite seventeen, whose narrow waist was encumbered with a heavy Navy Colt and who wore a second gunbelt loaded with bullets, bandoleer-fashion, around his chest. Soft-spoken, yet tough enough to keep up with this band, he was nevertheless wary of his companions. To Longarm it appeared he was out of his true element, a good kid trying not to show how good—or sensitive—he really was. This softness had long since been spotted by the other gang members, however, and they worked tirelessly to toughen the kid to their standards.

He had a shock of hay-colored hair and blue eyes that looked wider than they were because of his sunbleached eyebrows. His face was raw from the sun and his hair needed cutting. Though his shoulders were bony, they were already broad enough, and he rode a horse with the assurance of a Comanche.

The other two riders were Buck Masters and Slim Teller. They rode side by side mostly, and it was clear they had been trail buddies for a long while. As tough and reliable as old reatas, their faces were wrinkled and tanned to the consistency of old leather by the sun and dust of so many long trails, and their patience honed by not a few incarcerations, which they boasted of with some pride.

Buck was the taller of the two, with shiny black hair, eyes like gunbarrels, as silent as a snake, with a way of moving that was unhurried and calm, yet deceptively swift and decisive. It was as if the outlaw had spent his entire life figuring the quickest and most effortless way to accomplish all those minor tasks that clutter men's lives.

Slim—a long, lanky, cadaverous man—was Buck's polar opposite, a fuming, cursing, bumbling disaster. If he did not get tangled up in his reins before mounting, he would be holding up everybody while he looked for his halter rope or his canteen, sometimes even his horse. In short, Slim was a man who needed the compulsive neatness and decisiveness of Buck, while Buck needed someone like Slim to look after. They argued continuously, but it was a soft, gentle argument usually, more like two strange birds singing a song that comforted them.

And what really brought them even closer together was their fine, well-honed dislike of Red Larson.

As they dismounted in the cabin's front yard a young Mexican woman in her twenties appeared in the doorway. Behind her loomed a fat, dark-eyed Indian. The young Mexican woman—her eyes lustrous, her breasts full enough to push against the low-cut red blouse she wore—left the doorway and halted on the low porch, one hand reaching out to one of its posts.

28

"Bat!" she said. "What took you?"

"Had business. Les been here?"

"Nope. Ain't seen him."

He nodded, dismissing her, then turned to face Longarm directly. "You and the Kid sleep in the horse barn tonight. There ain't no more room for you in the bunkhouse."

Longarm glanced at the bunkhouse and breathed a sigh of relief. It was made of rough-cut logs, a low, untidy affair with only two windows in the front and a roof that, from the looks of it, probably leaked. Longarm much preferred the barn.

"Come on, Kid," he said. "Let's find us the hay mow and some fresh hay."

"Suits me," said the Kid, leading his horse toward the barn.

As he walked, Longarm saw the Kid glance twice over toward the young Mexican woman, who was still standing on the porch, watching him and Longarm heading for the barn. The woman caught the Kid's second glance and sent him a quick smile, then looked casually away. The Kid glanced about to see if anyone had caught her smile, his face blushing crimson. When his eyes met Longarm's, he knew that Longarm had seen it. He looked quickly away.

After they took care of their horses, they looked around for some fresh hay. There wasn't any. Not fresh, anyway. But what they found was clean enough. Using a rusty pitchfork, they shook out the dead grasshoppers and built themselves each a bed in the loft, near a large, open window. When they finished, Longarm sat on the edge of the loft and, ignoring the hay dry as tinder on the floor below him, lit a cheroot and took a deep, grateful drag.

29

The Kid came over and looked hungrily at the cheroot. Without a word, Longarm handed him a cheroot and lit it for him.

"Be careful with that butt," he told the Kid.

"Sure. Thanks, Jed."

"Who's the Mex filly?"

"Her name is Consuela."

"Lovely name."

"She's Bat's woman," the Kid said unhappily.

"That so?"

"But she likes me. Very much. That's why I stay with this gang."

"You going to rescue her from Bat?" Longarm asked.

"I don't know what I'm going to do," the Kid said miserably.

Longarm looked at the Kid. He was serious. He frowned and looked away. "You know what, Kid?"

"No, what?"

"You already told me too much."

"I can trust you."

"How in hell do you know that?"

The Kid shrugged.

"Well, you're crazy. Keep your mouth shut around me—and around the others—or you'll likely end up with a bellyful of hot lead."

"You threatenin' me?" the Kid asked, bristling.

"No. I'm warning you. Keep your feelings to yourself. And especially when they get tangled on Bat Coulter's woman."

"Then you don't believe she likes me."

"That's right. I think she may be having a little fun with you. But I don't care, one way or the other, Kid."

"You tellin' me I'm a fool. You sayin' I don't know when a woman's sweet on me?"

30

"As a matter of fact, Kid, I don't think you know enough to get in out of the rain. Are you sure you're dry behind the ears?"

The Kid bristled. "You watch out, Jed. I might get angry."

"What'll you do? Shoot me?"

"I'm warning you. I'm pretty fast on the draw."

Longarm laughed, enjoying himself hugely. "Prove it."

The Kid went for his gun. Still laughing, Longarm slapped the gun to one side, grabbed the Kid's wrist with his other hand, and twisted the big Colt out of his grasp. Still puffing on his cheroot, Longarm emptied the cartridges into his palm, handed the empty weapon back to the Kid, then leaned over and dropped the six cartridges into the Kid's side coat pocket.

"Better watch that, Kid," he drawled. "Shouldn't load all six chambers. Use the empty one to rest your hammer on. You're liable to blow off your foot with the hammer resting on a loaded chamber like that."

Moistening his lips, the Kid nodded, astonished that drawing on Longarm had not angered the man at all. He had treated it lightly as a game. The Kid broke open his sixgun and reloaded, this time slipping in only five cartridges, then carefully resting his hammer on the empty chamber before dropping the sixgun back into his holster.

"I'm hungry," Longarm drawled. "Is that Indian a good cook?"

The Kid nodded quickly. "Sure enough is. She's the best damn cook in these parts."

"That ain't sayin' much. This is pretty isolated country."

The triangle started clanging. The two dropped

31

lightly to the barn floor and hurried across the yard to the log cabin.

Standing in the bedroom doorway, Consuela lying face up on the bed behind him, Bat Coulter watched Longarm and the Kid file in and take their places at the big table. They were as ravenous as the others, and Little Salmon had to hop to keep their plates full. They had entered smoking cheroots, he noticed. Something about that fact alerted him, but he did not know to what. He shrugged uneasily. There was something about this Jed Morgan that bothered him, something in his manner that galled him. He stood too tall for his own good. Or was it more than that?

Something tucked away deep in his memory kept nagging at him. At times he would almost have it clear in his mind what it was, and then it would be gone. Well, it would all come out in the wash. As soon as they took that train. Then he'd wipe the slate clean of every single one of these animals and take Consuela to San Francisco—and ports east. He smiled at the prospect and turned to Consuela.

She smiled back. "Close the door," she told him.

He kicked it shut, advanced on the bed, and looked down at her. "Take off your blouse, then your skirt."

Tiny flecks of light danced in her eyes. "The men are just outside in the next room. They'll hear us."

Bat laughed. "Let them. Make 'em jealous—especially the Kid. You got him crazy already."

She smiled, her teeth sparkling in her round dark face. "Yes. He is so easy. Sometimes I feel sorry for him."

As she spoke, she pulled up her blouse and flung it

over her head, revealing her large, melon-shaped breasts. Swearing softly under his breath, he swiftly unbuckled his pants and stepped out of them, then flung off his shirt. Dropping onto the bed beside her, he rested his big hand on her inner thigh and moved it up under her skirt. She gasped as he discovered she was wearing nothing at all under the skirt. With one quick movement, he ripped the skirt from around her waist and mounted her.

"Hey, you too quick!" Consuela protested.

She pushed him back off her. Furious, Bat slapped her hard.

"You peeg!" she cried, slapping him back. Before he could protect himself, she pulled him close and sank her sharp teeth into the soft flesh just above his clavicle.

Groaning, he punched her so hard, she rolled off the bed, slamming down on her back. He looked down at her, grinning.

"You ready now?"

"It's a little better now, I admit," she told him, her eyes glowing with the excitement engendered by their fight. "But first maybe I kick you in the balls."

"Come ahead," he dared her.

She leaped up off the floor and rushed him. He caught her and the two went flying across the bed, landing on the floor on the other side of it. He came down on top of her, bent his head quickly, and bit her back. She screamed tightly, then punched him in the right kidney, an old trick of hers. He gasped painfully and raised up. Seeing her chance, she lashed out at his crotch with her foot. But he had expected that move and pulled back just in time. Grinning, he regained his feet and retreated to a neutral corner, the blood from her bite streaming down his sweaty chest. He was fully erect now, a raging bull eager for her, and he could tell from the look in her flashing eyes and the dark flush that covered her face that she was in the same condition. It was time to end foreplay the way they always did. With a happy roar, he went for her.

At that moment the door burst open. The Kid rushed in, sixgun in hand. One look at the disheveled Consuela sitting up on the floor beside the bed as Bat Coulter charged her, and he came to a conclusion as obvious as it was wrong.

Holding up, Bat spun to face the Kid. "What the hell—"

"Unhand her, Bat!"

"You outa yore mind, Kid!"

The Kid thumb-cocked his revolver. "You heard me, Bat. Leave Consuela alone."

"Why, you meddlin' little punk, I'll have your ass in a sling for a week!" As he spoke, he advanced on the Kid with no regard at all for the revolver in his hand.

"Bat!" Consuela cried. "He's got a gun!"

This cry of warning—from Consuela to Bat—startled the Kid, who a second before had thought he was on a white horse charging to Consuela's rescue. Bat saw the sudden bewilderment on the Kid's face, but it did not make him pause.

That was when Longarm joined the party. Before Bat could reach the Kid, Longarm spun him around and caught him a solid punch flush on the jaw. The Kid's knees sagged. Longarm followed up with a quick slam to the Kid's gut. As the Kid sagged forward, Longarm deftly took the Kid's gun from him, then flung him over his shoulder and lugged him out of the bedroom.

"Good riddance," said Bat, slamming the door. He turned to Consuela. "You got the Kid hooked, all right. Hell, he damn near put a bullet in me."

"Never mind that fool," she said, flopping quickly up onto the bed. "If that Morgan hadn't stepped into this, you mighta killed the Kid, the way you were workin' him over. What's the matter with you? He was just trying to save my honor."

"Your *honor!* That's very funny, Consuela."

She bristled.

He reached over and took her by the hair. "Ain't it?"

"Yeah, sure," she agreed grudgingly. "Come on. I'm ready now, damn you. Ain't you got somethin' you want to put inside me?"

With a happy roar, Bat dove onto the bed and slammed into her. Consuela grunted with pleasure, wrapped both arms around his bullish neck, and hung on, grinning. . . .

Much later, Longarm heard light footsteps on the ladder leading to the loft. He closed his right hand around his Colt and opened his eyes just enough to see the top of the ladder. It was very dark and he could not be sure, but he thought he caught the gleam of Consuela's dark hair, and a glint of brown flesh that must be her shoulder. Then he heard her moving through the hay toward him.

Longarm pushed himself up onto his elbows. "What're you up to, Consuela?"

"Don't you know?" she asked, her voice deeply seductive. Despite himself, Longarm felt shivers run up his spine. He did not wonder that the Kid was hopelessly confused where this wench was concerned. With-

35

out another word, she rolled back Longarm's tarp and snuggled in under it. As she pressed herself against him, he noticed she had pulled her skirt up past her waist and that there was nothing but her under it.

"We will have to be quick," she said. "Bat thinks I come over to tease the Kid."

She reached down boldly and grabbed his awakening erection. But he flung the tarp off her and stood up.

"What you need is a good spanking, Consuela."

"You do not want me?"

"I might get a disease."

She slapped him. He did not slap her back. Instead he flung her over his shoulder, and while she beat furiously on his back, carried her down the ladder, across the yard, and on into the cabin. Kicking open Bat's bedroom door, he flung Consuela down on the bed beside her lover.

Bat was sitting up with his back to the headboard, a bottle of whiskey in his right hand. He looked first at Consuela, then at Longarm. "What the hell . . ."

"Consuela tried to rape me," Longarm explained. "But I was able to hold her off. Put her on a leash, will you?"

Consuela flung herself off the bed and ran at Longarm. She was unable to scratch his eyes out, so she attempted to kick him in the crotch. He caught her wrists in his powerful hands and flung her back onto the bed. She landed in Bat's lap. He grabbed her, a grin on his face.

"Get out of here, Morgan. I'll take care of Consuela."

"I'd sure appreciate that." Longarm turned and strode from the bedroom.

• • •

The Kid was sitting up waiting for him.

"It sure ain't easy getting any sleep around here," Longarm remarked, slumping down onto his tarp.

"I been thinkin'."

"Don't burn yourself out."

"You're right. Consuela was just leadin' me on so Bat would have an excuse to kill me."

"That's the way I figure it."

"So you beat him to it. You punched me out to save my life."

"I admit, it *does* sound pretty drastic."

The Kid shook his head in bewilderment. "But what's Bat got against me?"

"You don't fit into his plans. With you gone, everyone gets a bigger share of the pie."

"Then why'd he let you join up with us?"

"Maybe he figures I'll be more use to him."

"That son of a bitch."

"Kid, you got any idea when we're going to tackle that train everyone's been talking about?"

"Soon's Les gets here."

"What's so important about Les?"

"He's the one handles the dynamite."

"Dynamite?"

"That's right. From what I hear, he's a real Chinaman when it comes to that stuff."

"I'm tired, Kid. Let's get some sleep."

As Longarm watched the Kid settle back into his soogan, he thumb-cocked his revolver and kept one eye open as he relaxed into sleep. This was one crazy bunch. And things would get even crazier when Les arrived and they began dynamiting trains.

Chapter 3

Longarm, perched on a ledge with the Kid a day later, was the first to catch sight of Lester as he rode through the pines toward the hideout. He turned to the Kid. "Go on back and tell Bat Les is on the way. I'll go down and meet him."

"He knows the way. You don't need to hold his hand."

"Just go on back and tell Bat."

With a shrug, the Kid turned and vanished back down the slope. Longarm waited for a moment until he heard the hoofbeats of the Kid's horse as he rode off. Then he got to his feet and angled down through the pines on a route calculated to intercept Lester.

When he stepped out onto the game trail a few yards ahead of the rider, Lester pulled to a sudden halt and glared down at Longarm. Lester's nose was still swollen badly. It resembled a small, round tomato. What bothered Longarm was that Les did not appear to be all that surprised to see him working as a lookout for Bat Coulter's gang.

"Bat will be glad to see you, Les. You got the dynamite?"

Les indicated the two boxes strapped to his saddle's cantle. "All we'll need."

"How's Serena, Les?"

Les shrugged. "What makes you think I'd care?"

"You mean you didn't go back to the ranch?"

"Hell, no. Good riddance."

Longarm did not believe Lester. The man had not been surprised to see Longarm planting himself in front of his horse. Only Serena knew Longarm had ridden off with Bat Coulter. And she also knew Longarm was more than likely a lawman. "All right, Les. How'd you know I joined up with Bat's gang?"

Lester's eyes shifted nervously. "I didn't know nothing about it."

"You're surprised as hell to see me, eh?"

"Yeah. I sure am."

Lester was lying. Longarm could smell it. He stepped around to the side of Lester's horse, reached up, and grabbed Lester's belt. Hauling him off his horse, Longarm flung him to the ground. He hit so hard he bounced.

"No bullshit, Les," Longarm snapped. "Did you go back to Serena's ranch?"

Shaking his head, Les stared blearily up at Longarm. For some idiotic reason, he reached back for his sidearm.

"Don't tempt me, Les."

40

Lester let his hand fall away from his gun butt. "You won't get away with this, mister. Bat ain't goin' to like this."

"Name's Morgan. Jed Morgan. And I don't care what Bat likes. Now, I'll give you one more chance. Did you go back to the ranch?"

Lester moistened his lips. "What if I did?"

Longarm hauled Lester to his feet. "Well, I'm warning you, Les. If you put a hand to Serena, I'll be coming after you. And you can count on that."

"She's my wife!" Les blustered. "You got no right to meddle between us."

"Then you did work her over?"

"Why not? I told you! She's my wife, not yours."

Longarm punched him in the face, knocking him back against his horse. The horse spooked and danced away and Les tumbled to the ground. Staring fearfully up at Longarm, Les began to wriggle backward. Grabbing the horse's bridle, Longarm pushed it aside and advanced on Les. In a panic, Les clawed for his sixgun, firing up at Longarm. Longarm ducked. The bullet whined past Longarm's neck as he lashed out with his boot, catching Les on the side of the head. Les flipped over and lay still. Longarm bent beside him, then flipped him over. He was still alive, but solidly unconscious.

Longarm approached the skittish horse carefully, grabbed the halter, and spoke softly to it. Once he had gentled it, he pried open the lid on one of the boxes. Probing carefully in the sawdust, he removed six sticks of dynamite and hid them in a hole he dug with his hands behind a large pine a couple of yards up the slope. Returning to the horse, he used the butt of his

41

revolver to tap the lid on the wooden box back down, then hauled Les upright. He was still groggy. Longarm slapped him smartly on the face until he was fully conscious.

"I'll tend to you later, Les," he told him, shoving him toward his horse. "Now get on up the trail. Bat's tired of waiting for you."

Glaring balefully at Longarm, Les hauled himself into his saddle, then urged his mount on up the trail. Longarm watched him go for a moment or two, then cut straight up the slope through the timber.

When Longarm reached the cabin, Bat was standing in the doorway with Lester. He did not look happy. As Longarm came to a halt in front of him, Bat pulled his hat down firmly and cleared his throat.

"What's the idea you working Les over, Morgan?"

"I don't like him messin' with Serena."

"Serena's his wife."

"Not if she don't want to be."

"Aw, hell," said Bat, turning to Les with a shrug. "This here ain't none of my business, Les. You two'll have to settle this some other time. Right now we got some plannin' to do." Bat looked at Longarm. "Get in here, Morgan. We're pullin' out tonight and we got a train to rob."

Consuela kept the coffee coming as Bat outlined his plan. With the gang members crowding around him, he used the table and various pieces of crockery to make his points.

Planting a sugar bowl down in the center of the table, he said, "This here's the north face of White Horse

42

Canyon." Alongside it he placed down a fork, then a salt shaker and a pepper shaker at either end. "The fork is the tracks, the salt and pepper, the trestles. Once the train passes the first trestle, Les'll blow the trestle ahead of it. That'll stop the train. The engineer will think maybe he can back up, but then Les'll blow the trestle behind him, and the train will be trapped. It won't be able to go forward or back."

"It'll just sit there, ripe for the picking," Red noted approvingly.

"And we'll be inside the train," said Buck, "ready to make our move. Right, Bat?"

Bat grinned at him. "Where else? And as soon as we get the drop on the postal clerk and whatever guards are on this shipment, we'll start loading up the pack horses."

"Who's bringing them?" Longarm asked.

"Consuela."

"Let me get this straight," said Longarm. "Les is going to blow *both* trestles? Suppose the train can't stop in time?"

"I know White Horse Canyon. I took the train through it twice. The engineer can see that second trestle long before he gets to it. He'll have plenty of time to stop."

"We got enough men to hold the passengers tight while we unload?" Red asked.

"We got enough, I figure, long's no one lets things get out of hand."

"You hear that, Slim?" Red Larson said, turning to address the man harshly. "You got to stay awake. You think you can manage that?"

"Lay off Slim," Buck told Red Larson, his voice

43

dangerous, "or you won't be making the trip at all."

For a moment it looked like there'd be trouble, but Larson grinned and backed off, shrugging. "Just so long as Slim stays awake. If he does that, I got no complaints."

Longarm spoke up again. "You mean we're just going to leave the train and its passengers stranded there when we get done?"

"Sure," Bat snapped. "You want us to take it with us?"

"You do this and you'll arouse the whole country," Longarm pointed out. "That's a long way back for those tenderfeet, over rough country."

Bat was astonished at Longarm's concern. "Christ, Morgan, what the hell do you care? We're robbing a train, not havin' a tea party."

Red chuckled. "Let the poor bastards walk back. If they're up to it."

"Jed's right," insisted the Kid. "We got to think of them tenderfoots. And the women and children."

"What's the matter with you two?" rasped Red. "You tryin' to weasel out of this?"

"Hell, no," replied the Kid hastily. "I was just askin', is all."

"Don't ask, then. Don't ask a goddamn thing. Just keep your mouth shut and listen."

The Kid bristled. "I don't have to take that from you, Red!"

Red grinned and rested his hand on his gun butt. "Who says you don't?"

"Lay off him, Red," Longarm warned.

"Shut up! All of you," snapped Bat. "Save the fight for the job ahead of us." He turned to Les. "You goin'

44

to need help planting them charges?"

"Nope."

"How you settin' them off?"

"With my rifle. Like before."

Bat nodded, but it was clear he was not entirely satisfied.

"Is Les that good a shot?" Longarm inquired mildly.

Les glared at Longarm. "Just keep out of this, Morgan."

"Well, if you ain't that fine a shot," Longarm drawled, "we'll all be getting a real nice view of the mountain scenery as we head for California."

"Morgan's got a good point," said Bat. He looked at Buck. "Buck, maybe you better go with Les, just in case. Outside of Les, you're the best shot here."

Buck nodded obediently.

"Damn it, I told you," Les said to Bat, "I don't need no help to set off them charges. I never have before."

"Shut up, Les. Buck's our insurance policy."

Les looked across the table at Longarm. His glance contained enough venom to kill a grown man.

"Hey, Bat," Slim asked eagerly, "what's on the train this time?"

Bat stepped back and grinned, looking very much like the cat who had just swallowed the canary. "Guess it won't hurt none to tell you," he allowed. "That mail car's goin' to be carryin' a consignment of gold bricks and dust for the mint in San Francisco, and more paper money than we'll know what to do with. The way I see it, after this heist we won't have to work for a living any more."

Slim turned to Buck, grinning eagerly. "Hey, Buck! Looks like we're gonna buy that ranch in Montana!"

"Maybe so," agreed Buck, just as pleased.

Consuela moved close behind Bat and snaked her hands around his waist. "Afterwards," she said, hugging him, "Bat and I are going on an ocean voyage. Ain't we, honey."

"Shut up, Consuela," Bat said. "Just keep the coffee coming."

It was obvious Bat was not happy that Consuela had revealed their plans. None of the other gang members appeared to notice, however; they were too intent on their own plans once they took their share of the loot.

"I don't like it," said the Kid.

They were approaching the barn. The full moon was high. The barn's great open doorway yawned ominously before them. Longarm held up, handed the Kid a cheroot, and lit up. The two drifted over to the pole corral. Leaning back against it, they smoked in silence for a while.

Then Longarm spoke up. "You don't like the idea of this train robbery, especially abandoning the passengers like that."

"I guess that's right, Jed."

"Then what're you doing here? What'd you think this gang did for a living?"

He shrugged. "I guess I didn't give it much thought at the time I joined. I wasn't thinking straight, I guess."

"Consuela?"

The Kid nodded miserably.

"Do you still—?"

"Naw," the Kid broke in. "That's over. She's Bat's woman. I know that now. I was a fool."

46

"Yes, you were. But most men are when it comes to women."

The Kid said nothing for a while. Then he took a deep drag on the cheroot and pushed himself away from the corral. "You're right, Jed. I really don't want to rob this train."

"I didn't figure you did."

"What about you?"

Longarm shrugged. "I guess I feel the same way."

"So why don't we pull out?"

"I was thinking of it, I admit."

"Then why don't we?"

"It isn't as simple as that."

"What do you mean?" the Kid asked.

"I mean we can't just pull out and let them go ahead and do this."

"So what do we do?"

Longarm took a deep drag on his cheroot and looked closely at the Kid. "I have a plan. You game?"

"Sure," the Kid said eagerly. "Let's hear it."

"When we get to Red Cliff, instead of boarding the train, we turn the gang in."

"Turn them in!" the Kid was astounded.

Longarm nodded. "To the sheriff."

The Kid pushed away from the corral fence and looked at Longarm. "Jed, you a lawman?"

Longarm hesitated only a moment. Then he nodded.

"Jesus! All this time my pardner's a lawman."

"You still game?"

"Just the two of us against the whole gang?"

"If we get the drop on 'em, it'll be a cinch."

"I—I don't know, Jed. It sure sounds dangerous. It's

47

Larson I don't like. He's worse than Bat. I think he's loco. We'd never get him to go quietly."

"No, maybe not. But I hid some dynamite. Once we get hold of it again, we'll be able to handle all of them without any trouble. A bullet won't scare some, but I never knew a man who wasn't afraid of being blown to pieces by a stick of dynamite."

"Where is it?"

"Hid. We'll pick it up when we ride out of here. You with me?"

"I'm with you."

Standing by the window, Bat frowned. He was concentrating so hard he was almost in pain. What bothered him was that gold watch and chain looped across Morgan's vest. And his cross-draw rig. Something about that troubled Bat, reminding him dimly of what he had once heard in Yuma about a federal marshal. Bat couldn't remember for absolutely sure how the watch and chain figured in it—but there it was, caught in his mind, like a bone in his throat. He couldn't swallow it and he couldn't spit it out.

If Morgan *was* a federal marshal, he was pretty damn close to the Kid, it seemed to him. So maybe the two were in it together, the Kid and Morgan. It made a kind of sense. Besides, what the hell kind of a highwayman lost any sleep over the passengers on a stage or train? They were there to be robbed and that was the beginning and the end of it. Bat sighed. The Kid and Morgan were loners, which meant he would have to kill them both if he was right. And he needed both of them for tomorrow's heist.

"What's the matter?" Consuela asked sleepily.

48

"I'm thinking."

She sat up and rested her back against the headboard of the bed. "Thinking?" she repeated sleepily, scratching her head. "Jesus, Bat. For you that must be a real strain."

She did not bother to cover her large breasts. He looked at her wide, erect nipples with no desire, so preoccupied was he.

"It's Jed Morgan." he said.

"Oh, that son of a bitch."

"Turned you down, didn't he? What kind of man would do that?"

"You tell me. You think he's queer?"

"Maybe."

"Jesus. If that ain't disgusting. The poor Kid. Maybe I was too rough on him."

"Tell you what. Go out and take the Kid on. Show him what a real woman can do for a man."

She blinked at him. "You serious?"

He grinned.

"What are you up to?"

"Tell the Kid you hate me and you want to run off with him. Hook him good and proper. Then find out what he knows about Morgan."

"About Morgan?"

"You heard me."

"But why?"

"Just do what I said."

"The Kid won't let me fool him again, Bat."

"Sure he will."

He was standing alongside the bed by this time. Reaching down, he hauled Consuela upright and cracked her in the nose with a fist. She went flying off the bed. When she hit the floor on her back, he kicked her viciously in the side. She squirmed onto her side, twisting in pain, blood flowing freely from her nose. Bat hauled her back up onto her feet, then shoved her toward the door.

"See what I just did to you? The Kid won't like that."

"You bastard!"

"That's right. Get real mad at me. It'll be more convincing."

"I think I hate you, Bat!"

He laughed. "You hate me enough to forget that sea voyage?"

She wiped her nose with the back of her fist and smoothed her dark hair back off her shoulders. "Some day you'll go too far with me, Bat."

"Some day, maybe. But not this time. Go out there and seduce the Kid. Find out what's going on with that big queer he's with. Maybe he's tryin' to foul up this raise I got planned."

"Afterward, you want me to bring the Kid over here?"

"Yeah. Good idea. Bring him over here so he can kill me for what I done to you."

Consuela opened the door and slipped out, dressed only in her long, tattered blue nightgown. As the outside door closed behind her, a shadow emerged from the next room and came toward Bat.

"What the hell's going on, Bat?" Red Larson asked.

"Come in here."

Larson followed Bat into the bedroom. Bat closed the door and, facing Larson, sat down on the edge of the bed. "It's Morgan. I got a funny feeling about that big

50

bastard, but I can't put my finger on it."

"What kind of feelin'?"

"Something I heard once about a federal marshal. It ain't clear in my head."

Red was alert on the instant. "You ain't makin' much sense, Bat."

"I know it, but it just ain't clear in my head. It's just a feelin' is all."

Red's mind began to race. "Well, now that I think of it, I didn't like that concern of his about the passengers."

Bat nodded quickly. "That's what got me to thinkin' too. Both of them could be up to something. We sure don't know much about Morgan and the Kid only joined us because he was after Consuela."

"Les hates that long drink of water's guts. He'd like nothing better than to slit him from crotch to brisket for movin' in like he did on his wife. Why not encourage Les to take him on?"

"Thing is, Red, I need Morgan. And the Kid. That's a long train we got to control. There's no tellin' who'll be ridin' on it. Maybe some fool soldiers or some crazy dudes with fancy rifles."

"So what you plannin'?"

"I sent Consuela after the Kid. When she gets through with him, he'll spill his guts willingly. We'll find out for sure then if Morgan and the Kid are on the level."

"You don't need all this fancy schemin' to find out. I could go over there now and beat it out of Morgan. Wouldn't take more'n ten minutes."

"It's just a hunch, Red. I might be wrong."

Without kicking off his boots, Bat settled back on the

bed, his arms crossed behind his head, grinning at Red.

"I wonder if Consuela's got the Kid's pants off yet."
He chuckled. It was a low, mean sound.

Red Larson shrugged and left the bedroom, stepping
past the sleeping forms of the other gang members.
Sometimes Bat was a bit too devious for Red's taste. If
Red was in charge, he would just walk over to that barn
and ventilate Morgan's skull, and that would be the end
of it. It seemed to Red that Bat Coulter was getting a
mite too fancy in his old age.

Before his bedroom doorway, Red pulled up. If this
Morgan *was* trouble, maybe even a federal marshal, and
the crazy game Bat and Consuela were playing didn't
get a handle on it, they'd all be in the soup.

Red had plans. After this raise, he had decided, he
was going to get himself a real tough bunch, men bigger
and more deadly than this collection of misfits. And
with this place as a hideout, he'd be able to last for ten,
maybe fifteen years. He and his men would become a
legend.

But he would sure as hell have a hard time rounding
up such a gang if he was holed up in Yuma for the next
twenty years. Turning away from his bedroom doorway,
Red slipped out of the cabin.

When Longarm saw Consuela's head appear just above
the loft floor, he closed his hand about the grips of his
.44 and waited. But this time, it appeared, Consuela
was after easier game. He heard her whimpering approach to the Kid and laid his head back down on the
saddle blanket. Before long, Consuela and the Kid
stopped talking and Consuela dropped beside the Kid.
The sound of Consuela's low, trembling voice quieted as

52

her seduction of the Kid proceeded.

Longarm did not close his eyes and did not relax his hold on the Colt's grips as he tried to figure out what Consuela was really doing up here or, more to the point, what deviltry Bat Coulter was hatching. It was certain he was the one who had sent Consuela on this mischievous errand.

The sound of thrashing ceased and Consuela's melodious voice sounded seductively. The Kid seemed out of breath. There was an extended discussion, low and intense, and Longarm heard the Kid's bootheels scraping against the loft floor as he pulled them closer to put them on. A moment later the Kid and Consuela left the loft together.

Bat's purpose in sending over Consuela was obvious. Bat wanted the Kid. He suspected Longarm and hoped the Kid would enlighten him. And, of course, the Kid could do that easily enough. Now that he was the recipient of Consuela's considerable favors, he would be more than willing to cooperate.

Longarm dressed swiftly while he cast about in his mind for whatever it could have been that had aroused Bat's suspicions. He came to light finally on his expressed concern for the train's passengers, a concern no reasonably hardened highwayman would have bothered to voice. He should have known better, Longarm realized. He should have kept his mouth shut. Even better, he should have cackled with glee as he and the others considered the stranded passengers' plight.

Clapping on his hat, Longarm dropped lightly to the barn floor, saddled his mount, and led it from the barn. Once he was out of earshot of the cabin, he mounted up and rode off through the moonlit night.

Close by the tree where he had hidden the dynamite, he was about to dismount when he heard a horse whicker behind him. Reaching for his .44, he turned. The pocked face of Red Larson loomed out of the night. Before Longarm could fling up his arm to ward off the blow, Larson's gunbarrel came down on his head. A second time it crunched down. Lights exploded deep inside his skull and he seemed to lose any power to resist. As he slipped crookedly off his mount, Larson's shadowy figure leaned out from his saddle as he pounded Longarm again, this third blow glancing off his skull and crunching painfully into his shoulder.

Longarm hit the ground. On his back he glimpsed the Big Dipper. Then Larson blocked it out as he peered down at the man he was trying to kill. Warm blood traced a path across Longarm's forehead and seeped into his left eye socket. His head throbbed dully as he passed in and out of consciousness. Strangely unconcerned about the possibility, he waited for Larson to level his gun and blow his fool head off. The entire scene was something he viewed from a great distance, feeling only mildly angry with himself for allowing Larson to take him this easily.

Larson dismounted, stepped closer, and lashed out with his foot, catching Longarm on the back of his head, just behind the ear. Longarm's head snapped around and his hat went flying. At the same time the gravel under the small of his back gave way and he felt his weight pulling him down a steep slope. The slick, pine-needle ground cover accelerated his plunge. He heard Larson curse, then scramble after him. Longarm began tumbling wildly. He crashed through some bushes, then plunged for a moment through space, coming to a bone-jarring halt wedged between a clump of juniper and a solid pine trunk.

Using his revolver, Larson pushed aside the juniper branches and peered down at Longarm. Longarm thought fast enough to allow his head to hang slackly while he stared without blinking up at Larson and at the pale moon's face hanging in the night sky just above his shoulder. Larson peered closer, studying Longarm's open, glazed eyes intently. After what seemed an eternity, Larson pulled back and holstered his gun and began pulling himself back up the slope. He did not look back and soon he vanished into the night.

Longarm waited until he heard the fading hoofbeats of Larson's horse before he began the painful task of hauling himself back up the steep slope. As soon as he made it to a level stretch, he crawled into cover under some bushes, then lay face down, doing his best to ignore the pounding in his head. Almost at once he lost consciousness. . . .

When he regained his senses, it was full daylight, well past noon. His head seemed three times larger than normal and there was a dim, persistent roaring in his ears. For a while he had difficulty focusing his eyes. Those fearsome blows to his head had resulted in a mild concussion, at least. In his condition, he was taking a chance just moving.

He caught sight of his hat on the ground ahead of him as he crawled out from under the bushes. He had no desire to place it down onto his blood-caked skull and carried it with him as he stumbled back to where Larson had overtaken him. His left shoulder and his arm protested whenever he reached out to grasp a sapling or take hold of a branch.

But he did not complain. He was damned lucky to be alive.

He found his horse calmly cropping the grass alongside a narrow stream, then returned to seek out the tree behind which he had hidden the dynamite. He found it with only a little difficulty and with extreme care packed the dynamite into his saddlebags, then mounted up and rode back through the pines. If Bat and his gang were still in the hideout, Longarm had an explosive surprise for them—and for Red Larson in particular.

But when he broke out of the timber onto the park leading up to the cabin, he saw that he was too late. It was completely dark by this time, the moon hidden by clouds, but the cabin was dark, with not a light showing. It was too early for the gang to have retired for the night; they must have already left for Red Cliff.

He considered trying to make it to Red Cliff to overtake the gang and, failing that, to alert the authorities; but he thought better of it and continued on toward the cabin. He was nearly done by this time. The persistent pounding in his head was getting damn near unbearable. He needed a safe place to hole up. Reaching the cabin, he left his horse in front of it without unsaddling it and stumbled through the door. A cot materialized in the darkness ahead of him. He slumped gratefully onto it and sank into a deep, exhausted sleep.

Caught in the shaft of sunlight streaming through the window, the Kid's body was turning slowly in the air above Longarm. The Kid wasn't dead. Not yet. Longarm jumped up off the cot and dragged over a chair. Then he cut the Kid down and placed him gently onto his cot.

The Kid's cheekbones had been shattered by repeated blows, a hole had been blown in his chest, and one arm hung uselessly from his shoulder. A few strands of muscle and skin were all that held it on to the rest of him. His neck and lower torso were encased with caked layers of blood. One of the men—Longarm was almost certain it was Red Larson—had carved opened the Kid's belly. Gray coils of blood-flecked intestines hung out of the incision.

The Kid opened his eyes and blinked uncomprehendingly up at Longarm. He tried to speak. Longarm leaned close, but he could hear only short, barely audible gasps. Longarm hurried over to the sink, pumped some water into a tin cup, and brought it over to the Kid, then held the cup to the Kid's lips until he had drained it.

This time the Kid spoke more clearly. "Larson . . . didn't he kill you?"

"He tried, sure enough," Longarm admitted. "He was close, but no cigar."

The Kid smiled; with his face broken up so cruelly, it was less a smile than a grimace. "Glad . . . " he rasped.

"Which of them did this to you, Kid?"

"Les . . . " the Kid gasped, "and Red Larson."

"Why?"

" . . . wouldn't tell them . . . about us . . . and what we planned."

"Hell, Kid. You should've told them!"

He shook his head. "Couldn't . . . do that. We was pardners . . . "

Longarm compressed his lips grimly, a scalding ache in his throat as he contemplated the Kid's ruined body.

"Get them for me, Jed."

"I will, Kid. That's a promise."

"They . . . laughed . . . while . . . did this to me."

"Even Consuela?"

"She was . . . worse. She . . . wanted them to cut off my . . ."

He began to cough and was not able to finish. It was a dry, wracking cough that should have brought up blood or fluid. Longarm went for more water, but when he returned to the cot, the Kid was dead—a merciful release.

Longarm looked down at the Kid. Badge or no badge, Bat Coulter's gang would pay for this.

Chapter 4

The guard was seated just in front of the door leading to the mail car, his chin resting on his palm as he gazed out at the passing scenery. A dusty deputy marshal's badge was pinned to his vest. His gunbelt had worked its way up his waist so that the Colt was not in a good position if he needed it in a hurry. Bat waited until the train clacked over the first trestle before he drew on the guard. The marshal didn't know he was in trouble until he turned from the window and saw Bat's grin—and the bore of his .45 yawning in his face. He made a half-hearted effort to go for his weapon. It was a foolish move. Stepping close, Bat pistol-whipped the man into insensibility while the passengers behind him watched in horror.

One passenger, a tall lean fellow in a plainsman's hat, got to his feet and reached up to the rack for his rifle. Red stepped out of his seat at the rear of the coach and shot the man between the shoulder blades. The sound of his gun's detonation filled the rattling coach with thunder and stunned the remaining passengers into terrified silence.

"Anyone else want to be brave?" Red demanded, his harsh, grating voice filling the coach.

There was no response.

Bat nodded, pleased. "Just stay in your seats," he told the rest of the passengers. "My men'll be around later to take your contributions. All we want is coin of the realm. Save your watches."

Bat turned and burst into the mail car. A small, wiry fellow wearing a green eyeshade was bent over a desk fastened to one wall. He turned at Bat's entrance, his mouth gaping in surprise. From behind the large honey-comb mail sorter stepped another marshal in the act of drawing his revolver. He should have waited a moment longer before stepping into view. Bat shot him in the chest, slamming him back out of sight. The postal clerk with the eyeshade shot both hands into the air.

Bat walked up to him and clubbed him on the top of his skull with such force he slumped to the floor without a sound. The dead deputy marshal was slumped against a huge strongbox. Alongside it sat a ponderous, squat black safe. Bat smiled. His information had been accurate. Gold dust in the strongbox, paper money in the safe.

He walked to the end of the car, pulled open the door, and peered up the tracks past the locomotive. He was just in time to see the trestle blow. It seemed to shudder; then it vanished into the gorge below.

The train shuddered as the sand hit the tracks and the

wheels locked. The high squeal of the flanged steel crunching over the sand and biting into the rails filled the air. So abruptly did the train slow that Bat was forced to grab the doorjamb to keep his balance. Yet closer and closer to the gorge the train squealed. For a moment Bat thought he had misjudged the distance it would take for the train to stop. Then the squealing faded as the train rolled gently a few feet more and came to a complete halt, the gorge gaping just beyond the cowcatcher. A powerful blast of steam came from the engine as the engineer vented his boilers.

Before the engineer could even consider going back, Les's rifle cracked once, then twice. On the second crack the trestle behind them blew. Watching the timbers break up and vanish into the gorge, taking the gleaming rails with them, Bat smiled. Les hadn't needed Buck, after all. But it had taken two shots to ignite the second charge.

He turned and walked back into the mail car.

"Open the door," he told the mail clerk.

Once it was open, Bat jumped to the ground. Slim Teller was already off the train, walking up the tracks toward him. When Slim reached him, Bat turned and walked up the tracks to the locomotive. The engineer and the fireman were leaning out of the window watching them, escaping steam from the panting locomotive shrouding them completely at times. Bat motioned to both of them to come down out of the locomotive.

"What do you need us for?" asked the engineer.

"To help us unload the gold."

The fireman, a hothead by the looks of him, glared angrily down at Bat. "Why the hell should we help you?"

"So we won't kill you."

Bat cocked his revolver. The engineer said something to the fireman and a moment later the two men climbed down out of the cab and proceeded sullenly back down the tracks ahead of Bat and Slim.

"Get up into that mail car," Bat told them as soon as they reached its open door. "You go first, Slim. I'll cover them from here."

Slim boosted himself up into the mail car, then turned and covered the two men as they clambered up after him.

Bat stepped back from the train, wondering where in hell Les was. Then he saw him, rifle in hand, a box of dynamite strapped to his back, scrambling down the slope to the tracks.

"Get up in there," Bat told Les as soon as Les reached him. "Blow the safe and the strongbox, then go back and give Buck and Red a hand. They got a whole trainload of passengers to pick clean."

"You see them trestles go?" Les asked, eager for Bat's approval.

"Sure did, Les. But it took two shots to detonate the second charge. Now get up into that train like I told you."

Somewhat deflated, Les clambered up into the mail car. Bat crossed over the platform between the mail car and the coal tender and jumped down onto the tracks on the other side. Peering past them down the steep, talus-littered slope, he saw Consuela. A tiny figure in man's dress, she was astride a roan, leading their mounts and a string of six pack horses. He waved. She caught sight of him and waved back. There was a narrow game trail leading up to the tracks which Bat had already checked over. He had told Consuela how to find it and was pleased to note that she was on it already. She would soon be up alongside the train.

So far, everything was going smoothly. Maybe too smoothly. It worried him. He turned and clambered back up onto the platform. That strongbox and safe could sure as hell slow them down some if Les did not blow it properly.

At least a mile before Longarm reached White Horse Canyon, he heard the two muffled roars indicating that Les had succeeded in blowing the trestles. He was close to the rim of the canyon when he heard two smaller, sharper explosions. When he reached the canyon rim, he peered down and saw the train halted on the narrow roadbed along the canyon wall, the trestles before and behind it blown clear. Bat, Les, and Slim—along with the fireman and engineer—were loading the gold onto a string of pack horses. They were packing the gold into aparejos, and under Consuela's watchful eye were doing a skillful job of balancing the heavy loads. The gold dust they were packing into ordinary packsaddles on their own mounts. So far, things appeared to be going nicely, and Longarm cursed himself for not having been able to prevent this.

Longarm had realized earlier that he did not have the time to ride to Red Cliff and intercept the gang before it got on the train there, so as soon as he buried the Kid, he had struck out directly for White Horse Canyon. On the way he had stopped at a settler's cabin; the settler, whose name was Jim Peel, had agreed to ride to Red Cliff to get the sheriff and a posse. But Longarm had little hope the posse would arrive soon enough to give him much help.

Returning to his horse, he tethered it in a small stand

of alders, then moved cautiously off the canyon rim with his Winchester and began the difficult descent down the nearly sheer canyon wall, being careful to keep out of Bat's line of sight.

There were four day coaches. The last two were Buck Masters's responsibility, and as the train ground to a halt, he stood up and announced his presence as well as his intentions to the passengers in the next to last coach. At that moment the conductor burst in from the rear coach waving a ridiculous .38 calibre Smith and Wesson. Before the idiot could discharge it, Buck slapped the revolver out of his hand, then clubbed him senseless to the floor.

This demonstration of Buck's resolve immediately quieted the passengers in both cars. On Buck's orders, every man with a sidearm was persuaded to dump his weapon out the window. For a while, the clatter of falling firearms filled the air. One man almost cried as he let drop his very fancy and quite expensive hunting rifle. With barely a mutter after that, the passengers gave over to Buck what valuables they possessed, apparently holding nothing back. At one point Buck gave way to an unaccustomed fit of gallantry and returned to one young lady a ruby brooch she tearfully offered him, then blushed uneasily at the gratitude that shone out at him from the woman's eyes. But from a whore in red mesh stockings traveling with a whiskey drummer, Buck took without a qualm a huge diamond ring, and from the drummer himself he confiscated a roll of greenbacks large enough to choke a Mexican mule.

Now, as he stood on the platform between the two coaches, watching Bat and the others loading up the pack horses, he felt pretty good. He had enough loot in his pockets to make him lean a little when he walked, and so far there had been no trouble, none at all. He sure had to hand it to Bat Coulter. When he planned a raise, it went off without a hitch.

Then he saw Jed Morgan.

High above him, Morgan was moving carefully down the steep slope. He was packing what looked like a Winchester. Raising his sixgun, Buck squeezed off a hasty shot. Morgan ducked back and out of sight as the bullet ricocheted off the face of a projecting boulder. Jumping to the ground, Buck raced down the tracks toward Bat and the others.

Red Larson had already left the train and was waiting for him as he ran up. "Who in hell're you shootin' at, Buck?"

"That gent you killed. Morgan!"

"You're crazy!"

"No, I ain't." Buck pointed to the almost sheer slope of rock and scrub pine slanting above them. "Go on up there if you don't believe me and take a look for yourself."

A puzzled frown on his face, Bat left Consuela and Slim and hurried down the tracks to join the two. "What's wrong?" he demanded.

"Buck says Morgan's up there."

Bat looked at Buck. "Morgan? That's crazy. Red killed the scn of a bitch."

"I tell you, he's up there," insisted Buck. "He's got a Winchester, and I don't think he's very happy."

Bat shaded his eyes and glanced up the slope. After a moment he said, "I don't see no one." He glanced at Red. "You think Morgan could still be alive?"

65

"I beat his head to a pulp, and when I left he looked done in to me—as dead as a doornail."

"I tell you I saw someone up there," said Buck, "and it looked like Morgan."

"You saw someone, maybe—but not Jed Morgan."

"All right," said Buck. "Let me and Slim go up and have a look-see."

"Do that," said Bat, "but hurry it up. We're moving out soon." He turned to Red. "Climb aboard and warn them passengers to keep their asses down and their heads inside. And if you get any lip from anyone, make him an example to the others."

Red clambered back up into the train and Buck moved on down the tracks with Bat. When he came up to Slim, who was busy packing gold bricks into an aparejo, he said, "Get your rifle, Slim. We're going hunting."

Slim straightened. Springy pieces of aparejo hay were plastered to his sweating neck and forearm. He mopped off his forehead with his bandanna and grinned in relief. "Sure thing, Buck. What's going on? One of the passengers break out of the train?"

"He thinks he saw Morgan," said Bat.

He moved on past the two men toward the mail car, where Les, a cocked sixgun in his hand, was keeping a close watch on the fireman and the engineer as they lugged out what gold dust remained in the blown safe. Consuela was busy tightening the aparejos' cinches on those horses already loaded with gold ingots and seeing to the wide, crupper-like breeching under their tails.

Watching Bat go, Buck shrugged and scratched his forehead in some confusion. "Guess he don't put much store by what I saw," he remarked to Slim.

66

"I don't care," said Slim. "I'm sick of loading them gold bars."

"Let's go, then," responded Buck, unlimbering his sixgun and heading for a sloping trail that led up behind a massive boulder. "I saw someone, damn it—and I'm ready to swear it was Jed Morgan."

Behind him, hurrying up the steep trail, Slim stumbled. From below them raucous laughter came from Bat and Les, who had been watching them. Buck felt his face redden. They thought he was crazy—that he was on a wild goose chase—and they wanted nothing better, it seemed, than to write both him and Slim off as a couple of jokes.

He reached down and yanked Slim up onto his feet. "Damn it to hell, Slim," Buck rasped. "Stay on your feet, at least."

His face straining from the effort to keep up, Slim said, "I'm doin' the best I can, Buck."

"Do better, damn it!"

Slim nodded dumbly, crestfallen as usual whenever Buck revealed irritation with him. Instantly Buck was sorry for having spoken as he had. He turned and pulled himself swiftly up the steep, gravelly slope. Reaching a level stretch on top of the boulder he had been climbing around, he turned and hauled Slim up after him.

As Slim straightened, Longarm stepped out onto the boulder, his Winchester held waist-high, a grim cast to his hard face.

"Oh, shit," said Buck, flinging Slim out of the line of fire and reaching for his Colt.

"Don't!" the lawman commanded.

But Buck was quick and he knew it. Crabbing sideways, he finished his draw and in one swift motion thumbcocked and fired. His round went wild, whining off a boulder beside Longarm. Dropping to one knee, with cool, almost reluctant precision, Longarm returned Buck's fire. Buck felt the hard impact as the round entered his chest. It felt like a heavy, hot fist and he could not seem to get his breath. Dropping his Colt, he looked down at the bullet's entry point, but saw nothing except a neat hole in his shirt. No blood. Nothing. And then he felt the warm blood trickling down his backbone.

Jesus! The bullet went clean through!

Still he could not catch his breath. He glanced over at Slim, who was frozen into immobility, and felt a sudden overwhelming despair. Who would take care of that silly son of a bitch now? He toppled to the sloping surface of the boulder and began to roll.

For a fleeting instant he felt himself falling through space, then nothing else. . . .

"Don't you be so dumb," Longarm told Slim, swinging his rifle about to cover the cowering train robber.

"You killed Buck!" Slim cried.

"Drop your gunbelt," Longarm commanded.

But Slim did not appear to comprehend. The sudden extinction of his partner seemed to be too much for him. Instead of unbuckling his gunbelt, he turned and plunged back down the trail. But the ground under his feet was mostly loose gravel and shale. His booted feet went flying out from under him. He tried to grab hold of something solid, but his frantic, scrabbling fingers found nothing. Longarm rushed over and managed to grab one of Slim's wrists, but before he could haul the man up, a shot came from below, kicking up a small explosion of sand and gravel into his face, and Longarm was forced to duck back for his rifle.

As he picked up the rifle and levered a fresh cartridge into its firing chamber, he heard Slim's cry as he tumbled back down the slope. The cry ended abruptly. Crouching at the edge of the boulder, Longarm peered over and saw Slim's crumpled figure lying alongside the tracks not more than a yard from Buck's body. It must have been Red Larson who had just fired that shot. He was already halfway up the slope—a rifle in one hand, his Colt in the other—and when he caught sight of Longarm peering down at him, he lifted his Colt and flung another shot up at him.

Longarm ducked back away from the edge of the boulder and straightened up. He was still able to see the roadbed below him. The gunfire had alerted the passengers to the possibility of their getting caught in a crossfire and they were now spilling out of the train and scrambling back along the tracks to get out of the line of fire. The women were shouting frantically to each other, their voices shrill with panic. Some tripped and stumbled on the uneven cross-ties. Only the little girls and small boys seemed capable of negotiating the uneven tracks with any speed. The men, holding on to their hats and glancing furtively over their shoulders as they raced past the women and children, did not cut very heroic figures. Watching them, Longarm immediately lost interest in their fates. It was the women and children who mattered. If that posse he had sent the settler after ever showed up, they'd be all right.

Les, Bat, and Consuela, meanwhile, had mounted up and were moving off with their pack horses and their saddled mounts laden with gold dust. Even as Longarm watched, they disappeared beyond the nose of the still panting locomotive.

Leaving the boulder, Longarm scrambled up the

steep, treacherous slope for another hundred yards or so, then wedged himself in between a pine and a flat slab of rock protruding out from the canyon wall. From this vantage point he had an unobstructed view of the slope clear down to the tracks and beyond. With Consuela in the lead, Bat Coulter and Les were already halfway down the far slope to the canyon floor, their gold-laden pack horses in tow. It seemed that Bat and what was left of his gang were not going to wait to see how successful Red Larson would be in finishing off—this time for good—one Jed Morgan.

Longarm peered down the slope, waiting for Red to appear. But he did not show himself. When he did come in sight, he was well off to Longarm's right, scaling a flat rock, and before Longarm could get off a shot he vanished behind an outcropping of scrub pine. It would only be a short while, Longarm realized, before Red would be above him.

Longarm scrambled the remaining yards up to the canyon rim and was just in time to catch a glimpse of Larson ducking into a stand of pine farther down. As Longarm, ducking low, darted across a small clearing, Larson opened fire on him from the timber. Puffs of dirt kicked up in front of Longarm a second before he gained cover behind a huge boulder.

Once behind the boulder, Longarm sent a few rifle shots into the timber. Larson returned the fire, peppering the face of the boulder with a steady fusillade. Longarm was safe enough behind the boulder, but once he left it, he would be in plain sight—and Red Larson would have a clear shot. It was, at least for the moment, a stalemate.

Longarm cursed.

He did not like the way things were going—or had gone, for that matter. Fortunate enough to stumble on the Coulter gang in the first place, his luck had been bad from that moment on. Now, unable to prevent the train robbery, he was pinned by this son of a bitch while Bat and the remainder of his gang made off with the loot. If this sort of thing continued, he might be well advised not to return to Denver and Billy Vail's justified scorn —or, worse, his sympathy.

Longarm's mount was tethered in some alders off to his left, on the far side of the clearing. Halfway between the boulder and the alders there was a thick clump of berry bushes. They were thick enough, but they offered precious little cover. Still, it was all Longarm had if he were to end this stalemate. He crouched just to the right of the boulder and began to send a steady fire into the timber about where he assumed Red was still crouched.

Then, abruptly, he ceased firing, turned and dashed out from the other side of the boulder, and legged it to the bushes. Flinging himself down behind them, he lay flat and waited for Larson to open fire. He did not have long to wait. Firing a steady fusillade, Larson's rounds clipped through the bushes just above Longarm's head, showering his head and shoulders with tiny shards of leaves and branches. Keeping his head down, Longarm peered through the bushes for gun flashes. When he caught sight of them, he opened up with his Winchester, driving Larson back deeper into the timber, ending the man's fusillade. Jumping up from behind the bushes, Longarm raced across the clearing and into the clump of alders.

His horse, skittish from all the gunfire, reared un-happily at his approach. Reaching out, he grabbed the horse's bridle and gentled him with soft words as he patted his trembling neck. After a short while, the horse quieted and Longarm went to one of his saddlebags and opened it. Carefully he withdrew one stick, then tied down the saddlebag, and hurried back toward the timber where Red was still crouched.

He was in time to see Red emerge from the timber and start to sneak across the clearing after him. In plain sight, Longarm flung himself flat. Realizing he was in Longarm's sights, Red pulled up, ducked aside, and legged it back toward the timber. Longarm flung the stick of dynamite. It landed behind the running man and skittered along the ground, almost catching up to him. Longarm fired two quick rounds at the dynamite. His second bullet caught the stick a second before Larson would have vanished into the timber. The detonation was surprisingly powerful. All Longarm saw was a blinding ball of fire above which Red's body bounced high, loosely, like a rag doll thrown from a wagon.

Squinting through the dust, Longarm walked across the clearing, skirted the small black, smoking crater, and came upon Red Larson sprawled face up on the ground, a gathering puddle of blood oozing out from under his back. Red was alive, but only just barely.

His eyes flickered open. "You dirty son of a bitch," he rasped as he saw Longarm bending over him. "That dynamite cut me in two."

Longarm unholstered his Colt. "I'm pleased to hear that. Figure that as coming from the Kid. Now tell me, where's Bat heading with that loot?"

"Up your ass," snarled Red.

Longarm straightened. There was no reason now for Larson to cooperate. Besides, it was not in the man to

72

be helpful. Longarm cocked his Colt and aimed at a spot just between Larson's eyes.

"This one's for me, Larson," Longarm told him quietly.

"Go ahead, you bastard. Shoot."

Longarm fired.

Chapter 5

A moment later, as Longarm was mounting up, he heard a shout and saw a very fat lawman, his badge pinned to a dusty vest, approaching at full gallop, a line of weary riders strung out behind him. Longarm finished mounting up and rode to meet the man he assumed was the sheriff of Red Cliff.

"I heard an explosion!" the sheriff puffed. His beefy face was scarlet and he was mopping his forehead with a polka-dot bandanna as he yanked his mount to a halt alongside Longarm. "What's goin' on, mister?"

"Over there, near the edge of that timber, you'll find a dead man. His name is Red Larson and he's a member of Bat Coulter's gang which just held up a train. There's a big chunk missing from Larson's back and a neat hole between his eyes. A stick of dynamite fixed his back, a bullet from my .44 drilled the hole."

"Who the hell are you?"

"Custis Long, deputy U.S. marshal out of Denver. And who might you be?"

By this time the rest of the posse had reached them. There were thirteen riders in all, clerks and townies for the most part, with only a couple of men who looked capable of any sustained riding. They reined in at a respectful distance and formed a loose semicircle around Longarm and the fat man. All of them seemed weary, and it looked as if they had ridden their horses to their limit.

"I'm Sheriff Glenn Scott," the beefy fellow proclaimed, slapping his badge. "How do I know you're who you say you are?"

"Did a settler come for you, warning there'd be a holdup of the train at White Horse Canyon?"

"That's right."

"And his name was Jim Peel?"

"Yeah."

"Did he say who sent him?"

"Custis Long, a deputy marshal. But I still don't know if you're the same man who sent Peel."

"Then you'll just have to take my word for it, won't you."

"Don't you have any identification?"

"I lost it."

Scott tipped his head slightly as he regarded Longarm. "You *lost* it? Some lawman you are."

"Save the criticism, Sheriff. Marshal Billy Vail will take care of that much better than you. At the moment you got other business. There's a crowd of unhappy passengers down on the tracks behind me who are going to need help getting back to Red Cliff."

"What about the train robbers?"

"Three of them are dead. That one I mentioned a moment ago and two others near the tracks below."

"Where's the rest?"

"They got away."

"With the gold?"

"The gold and the money."

"Jesus. Wait'll they hear about this. You got any idea what we're talkin' about here, Long?" The sheriff, it seemed, had decided to believe that Longarm was who he said he was.

"A pretty large amount, I gather."

"Hell! I saw them loading it. We all did. From the Link Mine, it was, and Wells, Fargo melted down the gold into ingots for them. A king's ransom, it was. Mark my words, all the Eastern reporters'll be in town looking for a story."

"I repeat, Sheriff. Your job now is get help to those passengers who are stranded on the tracks."

"Yeah, sure. Maybe you better show us."

Longarm turned his mount, and with the sheriff and the posse following him dutifully, rode to the rim of the canyon and dismounted. The sheriff and the members of his posse got off their horses also and peered down. Below them was the stranded train, the engine still venting a little steam. The two dead train robbers were still sprawled where they had landed. And at the far end of the tracks, huddled close by the blown trestle, was a large, unhappy brood of civilians.

The sheriff studied the situation for a second or two, then turned to Longarm. "Just how the hell are we supposed to get down there?"

"Leave your mounts up here and go down on foot. Be careful. It's a steep descent."

"It sure as hell looks it. You could break your neck."

Then the big man sighed and looked around at the posse. "Guess we rode a long ways for nothin', boys," he called out to them. "The train got cleaned out and the gang's long gone, according to this gent. So all what we got now is a passel of unhappy men and women and squallin' kids to haul up here."

The men nodded sullenly and went back to their horses for ropes. Sheriff Scott looked carefully at Longarm.

"Where you headed, Long?"

"I'm going after the rest of the gang. Bat Coulter, Lester Gullick, and a woman called Consuela."

"Good luck."

"You got a pencil on you, Sheriff—and maybe a pad, too?"

The sheriff reached into his saddlebag and pulled out some old dodgers and a small stub of a pencil. Longarm took the pencil and on the back of one of the dodgers he wrote Vail a terse message, telling him he would be back just as soon as he caught up with the Bat Coulter gang—and the gold. Signing it, he handed the message to the sheriff.

"As soon as you get back to Red Cliff, send this telegram to Marshal Billy Vail at the U.S. Marshal's office in Denver."

The sheriff took the dodger from Longarm. "You goin' after these varmits alone, are you?"

"That's right, Sheriff, unless you have some men in your posse anxious to make the trip with me."

"There is one."

"Who is he?"

"Bob Rutger. His pa was killed by these train robbers last year when they robbed a train north of Denver."

"He's welcome to join me," said Longarm, "if he has a mind to."

"I'll go check with him."

Longarm watched impatiently as the sheriff walked back to one of the posse's members, a long, lantern-jawed fellow with a black, floppy-brimmed hat. He listened eagerly as the sheriff relayed Longarm's offer. The fellow glanced quickly over at Longarm and immediately nodded his agreement. Noting this, Longarm swung into his saddle and waited for his new deputy to remount and ride over to him.

When he had, Longarm introduced himself, the two shook hands, and then, without a look back at the sheriff and his posse, they headed out.

A week after fleeing the train with their string of heavily laden pack horses, Bat pulled his mount to a sudden halt and chucked his hat back off his forehead.

"Do you see what I see?" he asked Consuela incredulously.

All Consuela could do was nod. Beyond a bridge just ahead of them sat a strange little town nestled between the sheer slopes of this high mountain valley. It had narrow streets and buildings with curious-looking roofs, giving it a strangely alien cast and reminding Consuela of no other town she had ever seen in her life. Yet the place was not all that different from other small towns she had encountered in her travels with Bat. There was a saloon, small shops, a livery and blacksmith shop, a barbershop, and a general store at the far end of the main street. The strangeness, she decided, lay in the small touches, the narrow windows and the ornamentation around the doors. Most especially the curious way so many roofs seemed to curl up on their edges like hatbrims.

Les spurred his horse up alongside Bat's and grinned. "I heard about this town, Bat. Never did believe it, though. Chinks built this place. They wanted a town hidden away. They couldn't afford the passage back to China and couldn't take the hassle when honest workers took over in the mines and drove them out."

Consuela looked at him. *"Honest* workers?"

"Sure. Workers who wouldn't work for coolie wages."

"You mean the Irish," snorted Bat.

Les was Irish. He bristled. "You sayin' there's anything wrong with the Irish?"

Bat grinned at Les, enjoying his discomfiture. "I say they work hard enough—but maybe they drink just a mite harder."

"Stop squabblin'," Consuela said, glancing nervously up at a small, whitewashed building perched on a hill high above the town. It had very small, elongated windows. Its roof resembled a woman's bonnet, she decided. The building itself reminded her of a shrine or a church as it gleamed brightly in the slanting rays of the afternoon sun.

They had come upon the road they were on now a few miles back and it had led them across a wide marshland to this spot. They had had to be extra careful to see to it that none of their pack horses stumbled off the narrow roadway into the water. How deep the water was they had no idea, but they suspected that if any of their heavily laden pack horses plunged into the watery wasteland, it would be close to impossible to get the animal back on the road.

80

Ahead of them sat a curious bridge spanning a large open channel in the marsh. They would have to cross it to get to the town beyond. The carved wooden heads of four lions sat on pedestals at both ends of the bridge. The curved planking that made up the floor of the bridge had been laid down lengthwise, not crosswise, and appeared to be constructed of solid, square-cut beams. The bridge itself was supported by a complicated network of cantilevered struts upon which, on both sides of the main causeway, had been constructed pedestrian walkways. High up in this bleak, isolated stretch of mountainous country, this bridge was an impressive and solid example of workmanship.

"Well, let's get going," said Bat. "Maybe these Chinese'll have fresh horses we can borrow. Our horses are about done in."

They clopped over the bridge, its floor giving off a solid, booming sound, then continued on toward the town. The closer they got, the more obvious it became that the place had long since been abandoned: Windows were broken. The shutters on most were hanging crookedly. Doors had been broken in, and shattered remnants of them remained still in the doorways. Traces of loot hauled from the homes littered the streets: broken lanterns with curious, colorful shades, fragile bone china, crockery of all sorts, small black lacquered tables, most of them broken in half or their legs snapped off carelessly. The remnants of oriental rugs lay there, their colors almost completely faded, their fabric ground into the mud. Everywhere there could be seen scraps of curtains, silk dresses, scarves. Still, some of the houses were unscathed—in excellent repair, as a matter of fact.

As they continued on down the narrow main street,

Bat felt the hairs on the back of his neck stand up. He was being watched. He was certain of it. This town wasn't entirely abandoned.

"Hold it!"

The command came from Bat's right. He swung his head to see a bearded gunman and two of his sidekicks striding out onto the low porch of what once must have passed for a saloon. The three gunmen had unholstered their sidearms and were pointing them casually up at the three.

Shit! Bat said to himself. He and Les were out-gunned. If he didn't strike some kind of a bargain with this gunsel and his two sidekicks, he could say goodbye to his gold. But no—he'd die before he let anyone take this fortune from him.

A fourth man stepped out onto the porch. "Hey, Bat!" this one cried, grinning. "What'n hell you doin' up here?"

"Nate Heller!" Bat cried, a surge of relief sweeping over him. Heller was an old acquaintance, a fellow in-mate of his at Yuma not so many years ago. "You damn son of a bitch, Heller!" Bat cried. "What're you doin' up here without a leash?"

As Bat spoke, he dismounted, stormed up onto the porch, and grabbed Heller's hand with both of his. He pumped it once and then slapped the man on the back. Heller took the pounding good-naturedly and grinned back at him. On one miserably cold morning in Yuma, Bat had stepped between Heller and a mean, drunken guard intent on beating Heller to death. By absorbing as much punishment as Heller and thereby wearing the guard out, Bat was able to save Heller's life. Later, after careful planning, the two had contrived to kill the guard. Using small scraps of wire they had confiscated from the kitchen over many months, they hanged the son of a bitch from an open window. It had been a salutary warning to the other guards.

Heller turned to the big, bearded gunsel. "Put down your gun, Pete. I know this gent from Yuma. I'll vouch for him. What name you usin' now, Bat."

"Same one. Bat Coulter. I kinda like it."

"Bat, meet Pete Kroner."

Bat shook hands with Kroner, who then introduced him to the other two men. One was Hank Fletcher, the other Bim Sands. Both looked tough enough to eat nails with pure rust as a chaser, and they didn't bother with the formality of shaking Bat's hand. A wary nod was sufficient for them.

Bat heard a distant shot. A piece of the porch post disintegrated. Glancing up the street, he saw a Chinaman duck back into an alley, a smoking pistol in his hand. Two more shots followed, this time from across the street.

"Get inside!" Kroner shouted to them.

"What's goin' on?" Bat demanded as he stormed into the saloon after Kroner and the others.

"We can use this here town," Heller explained, kneeling beside a saloon window and peering out, "just so long as we can keep them damn chinks off our backs. We've killed close to an even dozen since we first hit the place. But the more we take out, the more of 'em come out of the woodwork."

"Damn it," said Bat anxiously. "What about my horses out there?"

Heller grinned at Bat. "We'll go out and bring 'em in."

"In here?"

Bim Sands laughed. "Sure. We'll trail 'em through to the kitchen out back. It's been our stable since we holed up here."

Bat grabbed Les and ducked out of the saloon, with Bim Sands and Heller following out after them. They led every horse in through the saloon and out into the kitchen fronting the alley behind it. One wall was down so the horses stood with their heads in the kitchen, the rest of them in the alley.

It took some time to unload each horse and stack the aparejos in a corner, then rub the weary horses down sufficiently. Pete Kroner, curious, pitched in with his men to help the unloading. When that much of it was done, he had a question for Bat.

"Maybe you better tell us what you're carrying in these here aparejos, Bat. They're mighty heavy for such a small load. Only thing I know weighs that much for that little heft is gold. Pure gold."

Bat knew there was no way he could hide what he was carrying. With a shrug, he said, "Sure. That's what it is. We got enough here to make us all millionaires twice over. Moment I saw you fellers, I had no intention of holding out. Hell, I'd just as soon you fellers throw in with me. Share and share alike, I say. I'm headin' for California, and I figure I could use some extra hands. We lost two when we robbed the train, and I got a feelin' a third ain't goin' to be showing up either."

Kroner looked at him. "You mean you lost three men?"

"Looks like it."

"Well now, I calls that a cruel fate." Kroner said, eyeing the pile of aparejos hungrily. "You lost three

84

men, but here's four more all ready and waiting to take up the slack."

"That's the way I look at it, too," Bat agreed. "But I'm the one in charge. This is my operation."

"Is it now?"

"Yes, it is."

Bat caught a glint in Kroner's eyes he didn't like. It reminded him of the way a cat looks just before he decides to stop playing with the mouse he caught. Bat glanced warily over at his old jailmate, Nate Heller. But Nate was busy inspecting Consuela, and she was busy looking him over, too. It wouldn't take much for her to change sides, Bat realized, and felt himself tightening with resolve. He let his hand drop to his side, his little finger resting on the holster's front seam.

"Where in hell were you goin' with all this sudden wealth?" Kroner asked him.

"West. There's a pass not far from here, twenty miles maybe. Just past it I got a place where we can hole up until the heat's off. Then we'll move out. I got plenty of wagons waitin' there and enough provisions to take me all the way to California."

"You know the way, do you?"

"Sure."

"So how come you came this way?"

"Didn't intend to—not until I saw the road. I figured it was going west and would make it easier on the horses."

"Never heard of this little China town, eh?"

"Nope."

"What'd you say the name of that pass was?"

"I didn't."

"Wouldn't be Lost Eagle Pass, would it?"

Bat shrugged. "Never heard tell it had a name. It's just a pass."

"Give it a little thought, Bat," Kroner persisted. "The pass I'm thinkin' of is pretty high—and it has a long ridge on one side topped with spruce. A stream with a bright pebble bed runs down the middle of it from a snowfield trapped in a valley to the right. You can see the trout in the stream real clear. Is that the pass you're thinkin' of?"

Bat felt sweat standing out on his forehead and crawling down his back. That was the pass, all right. Kroner knew the country as good as any Indian, it looked like. And now Kroner knew where it was and what Bat had already stashed there. He had given the man a real edge, and he looked more than ready to take it. All of a sudden Bat's stomach felt like a lead ball had dropped into it.

He cleared his throat. "Hell, Kroner, there's lots of passes like that up here."

"You mean you ain't headin' for that pass I just described?"

"No, I ain't."

"You know what, Bat? You're holdin' out on me. You ain't bein' truthful, and I take that as a real unfriendly sign." Kroner smiled sadly. "The fact is, there ain't no other way out of this basin if you're goin' west 'cept by Lost Eagle Pass. That ain't all. I seen that place of yours—a nice, roomy cabin high up, hid in a patch of scrub pine. With plenty of barns and a good-sized corral."

"All right," Bat admitted weakly. "So you're right. That's the pass. Only I never knew it was called Lost Eagle Pass."

Kroner grinned happily. "What's the matter, Bat? Don't you trust me?"

"Sure, I trust you, Kroner," Bat said, trying to fix a smile to his face. "Just about as far as I can throw my horse."

Kroner smiled, relieved at Bat's bluntness. He took no offense, it seemed. "Hell, Bat," Kroner said, smiling easily, "if we're goin' to work together, we got to trust each other. Can't see workin' with a pardner what don't trust you. Just don't make no kind of sense. Could be dangerous, too." Kroner looked over at Heller. "Ain't that right, Heller?"

Heller was deeply engrossed in conversation with Consuela. Startled, he looked quickly down at Kroner. "It sure is," he replied hastily.

Leaning against Heller, Consuela looked coolly, appraisingly, at Bat, an enigmatic smile on her face. From the way she looked at him, he might have been a chicken in a pot with the water beginning to boil. Bat let the palm of his right hand drift back over the outside of his holster while a single cold bead of sweat trickled down his spine.

"Hell," Bat assured Kroner, "we can work together. I know I can trust you."

"Do you, now? Still, it ain't a good idea to have two men leadin' a bunch. Might get things all fouled up. Ship can't have two captains. Didn't you say me and my boys could join up with you? That right?"

"Sure."

"And you said you'd be in charge."

"Hell, like I told you, Kroner, it's my gold, my pack horses. And I'm the one who led the gang what robbed the train."

"And lost three men doin' it, by your own admission."

"Damn it! That couldn't be helped."

"Maybe not, Bat, maybe not. But the thing is, I never could get myself to play second gun to any man. I'm funny that way. I run things or else I don't play."

"Suit yourself, then," Bat said, steeling himself. "You don't have to come with us. You can stay here if you want."

Kroner smiled. "But I don't want. I'm bein' shot at by Chinamen and there's no woman to quiet my fever when night comes." He glanced over at Consuela and winked.

Bat knew what Kroner was up to. Quietly, deliberately, he was goading Bat, forcing him to make a move for his weapon. Failing that, he was hoping Bat would break down and let Kroner take over. Bat knew this. He understood the man's reasoning perfectly. He would do the same thing were he in Kroner's place. Still, Bat had no intention of backing down to Pete Kroner.

"Listen, Kroner," Bat said gamely. "I told you. This here's our gold—Les and Consuela and myself. We're the ones stole it. You're welcome to come along if you want. But I'm in charge. And if that ain't good enough for you, stay here. Suit yourself. Won't be no skin off my nose."

"Well now, that's just what I'm going to do, Bat," Kroner said. "Suit myself."

Bat looked around at Les and Consuela for support —and saw Les move closer to Consuela, watching Bat with the same coolly appraising look as Consuela's. The two of them knew what was at stake here—that Pete Kroner was going to try to gun Bat down for the gold.

88

Bat swallowed, but his mouth remained dry. The show-down was coming and there was nothing he could do to prevent it. His hand resting on the butt of his revolver, he edged back, looking for Kroner's men. Out of the corner of one eye he glimpsed Hank Fletcher. But where the hell was that other one, Bim Sands?

Bat took another cautious step backward and for a desperate moment visualized himself turning swiftly and vaulting over the bar. Then he found out where Kroner's other sidekick was as the muzzle of Bim Sands's sixgun slammed cruelly into his backbone. Bat froze and let his hand fall away from his holstered gun. Bim reached out and lifted it from its holster.

Bim chuckled. "You lookin' for someone, mister?"

All thought of heroics vanished on the instant. Bat was close to wetting himself as Bim shoved his gunbar-rel still deeper into his back, nudging him roughly away from the bar and closer to Kroner. Kroner smiled and drew his weapon so quickly and easily it seemed to ma-terialize in his hands.

"Get on your knees, Bat."

Bim Sands shoved him brutally and Bat collapsed forward, his knees slamming painfully onto the saloon's wooden floor. Hunkering down in front of him, Kroner slammed the barrel of his sixgun into Bat's mouth, chipping off four of Bat's front teeth.

"I tell you what," Kroner said, thumb-cocking the big Colt. "I won't shoot you, if either your woman or your old friend Heller here, or this other gunslick ridin' with you tells me not to. Ain't that fair enough? All one of them has to do is speak up for you and my hand will be stayed. You have my word."

Turning his head, Bat looked desperately up at Les,

his terrified eyes pleading. Les looked away, scratching the back of his head. Heller raised his eyebrows and shrugged. His arm was around Consuela's shoulder. Watching Bat, Consuela leaned her body lasciviously against Heller. Bat stared up at her, pleadingly.

She smiled down at him, her white teeth glowing in her olive face, her large liquid eyes bright with hatred. "Hey, gringo!" she cried. "Now you goin' to die! How you like that? I remember every time you hit me— every time you swear at me and use me like a whore. You know what, Bat? You stink! You smell like all the horse barns in the world!" She glanced over at Kroner, her eyes venomous. "What you wait for? Kill the dirty son of a bitch!"

"No, Consuela!" came Bat's muffled cry. "No!"

Kroner pulled the trigger. Bat felt rather than heard the detonation as the .45 caliber bullet smashed up through the roof of his mouth, carrying him into perdition—the long scream of his soul fading in the limitless darkness of an everlasting night.

Kroner looked away from the spray of blood, brains, and tiny shards of skull bone that plastered the bar and stepped back to let Bat's lifeless body topple forward onto the floor. He saw Consuela hurrying up the stairs with Heller, her hand held up to her mouth, her face white as chalk dust.

When Heller saw Kroner watching him, he paused— as if Kroner could tell just what was in his mind. Grinning suddenly, Kroner holstered his weapon. He sure as hell could.

"Go on up and take care of her," he told Heller. "I'll be up soon enough. Comfort her fine sensibilities. Get her all nice and warmed up for me. You think you can do that?"

Heller nodded eagerly and vanished up the stairs after Consuela.

Kroner glanced at Les and then at the dead train robber at his feet. "You want to do anything about this, or are you plannin' on stickin' with us?"

Noting the ease with which Kroner had disposed of Bat, Les found he had scaled down his wants considerably. He would be happy enough if he could simply hang on to the gold dust in his saddlebags and ride out. There was more than enough wealth in those bags to maybe give him the chance to make it up to Serena. He hadn't left her very happy with him, that was for damn sure—but he was going to mend his ways from now on, and with this much gold to buy all the pure-bred stock Serena could want, he didn't see how she could possibly turn him away, no matter what Abe or anyone else said.

Moistening dry lips, Les replied, "All I want's what I already got in my saddlebags. Then I'll be ridin' out."

"Well now, that suits me fine, mister," Kroner told him, obviously pleased to be rid of him. "But before you go anywhere, what about that dynamite Hank tells me you're packin'?"

"Hell, you can have it."

"Why, thank you, mister." Kroner glanced at Hank and Bim. "It might come in handy before long."

"Take it then, and welcome." Les dried the palms of his hands along the seams of his trousers.

"Before you go," Kroner told him, "drag that stupid son of a bitch out of here. Consuela was right. He smells up the place somethin' awful."

Bim and Hank stepped back and watched as Les

grabbed one of Bat's boots and pulled him across the floor to the rear of the saloon. Kroner lost interest as soon as the corpse was out of sight. He turned and started up the stairs.

Heller must have got that Mex gal's juices flowing by now—and he would be just in time to take advantage.

It was the faint, very distant echo of shots that first alerted Longarm. It was the landscape's rugged, bleak familiarity that gave him pause next, especially the three towering mountain peaks looming just ahead. And when he caught sight of the familiar narrow roadway winding far beneath him across a broad upland marsh, he knew at once where he was.

A moment after Longarm pulled up to gaze down at the roadway, both men sighted a lone rider going back the other way. Longarm grunted and sat a little straighter in his saddle. From the loose way the distant rider slumped over his horse as he rode, Longarm knew at once who he was.

Lester Gullick.

Noting Longarm's reaction, Rutger expectorated a long black sliver of tobacco juice at a defenseless plant. "That rider down there," he drawled. "You recognize him, do you?"

"He's one of the holdup men, all right. Name's Lester Gullick."

"Do we take him?"

"I'm thinking on it."

Rutger frowned intently down at the distant rider. "He's out of range of my Winchester. We'd have to go back and find a way down to that roadway. We could make it if we hurry."

Longarm nodded without comment as he peered reflectively down at Lester. The son of a bitch had thick saddlebags, and was carrying little else. There were no pack horses, which meant no gold ingots. And if he was alone it meant, more than likely, that he had had some kind of a falling-out with Bat and Consuela. If this were so, those two remaining gang members now owned most of the stolen gold shipment. It was curious that Les would stand still for this, and for a moment Longarm seriously considered circling back to cut off the outlaw. But Longarm was after the gold shipment as well as Bat Coulter. Les would have to wait.

Longarm had no problem with that. He had a gut certainty where Les was heading right now: back to Serena. Her pull was too much for the lone outlaw to resist. Les was going back to his wife and her horse ranch. It would make an ideal hideout—if Serena would have him.

Rutger destroyed another bush with his tobacco juice and shifted impatiently in his saddle. "We goin' to sit up here and watch that bank robber ride away? He might be one of them bastards shot my pa."

"Yes, he might."

"Well?"

"You can do what you want," Longarm told him. "But right now, I got other business—that gold shipment for one, and Bat Coulter."

Rutger said nothing, though from the way he went to work on a new chaw, it was obvious he was deeply troubled by Longarm's decision. Still, Rutger made no effort to take after Lester. He was willing, it seemed, to let the lawman's decision stand. Not that it was all that easy for Longarm to sit his horse quietly and watch Lester ride on out of sight.

But as he had just reminded Rutger, it was the gold shipment and Bat Coulter that Longarm was after, and now he had a pretty good idea where Bat and Consuela were holing up—the same town Longarm himself had visited on an earlier mission. It was a town built entirely by Chinese coolies who had been driven from the nearby gold fields by those white workers who refused to work for the same wages a coolie would. The little town should be deserted now. The Chinese overlord who had managed things had been routed and the jade production which financed the town had been diverted to paying the coolies' passage back to China. At least that was how Longarm had left things.

Les vanished from sight. Longarm turned to Rutger. "There's a town up ahead."

"Up here?"

"It's called Celestial City."

Rutger looked at him narrowly. Maybe Longarm was trying to pull his leg.

"That road down there leads to it," Longarm continued. "Lester must have just left the place. I figure that's where Bat Coulter's holed up—him and the gold."

"You sure you ain't tryin' to kid me? I never heard of no Celestial City, not up here."

"How often you been up here, Rutger?"

He shrugged. "This is the first time."

"Then why don't you just take my word for it."

Rutger shrugged. "Okay," he said. "What'll we do? Follow that road down there?"

"We better not. It'll take us into the town, but Bat'll be watching. We'll go around and come in from the north. There's a trail leads through a narrow pass."

Rutger nodded, his shrewd eyes studying Longarm

closely. "That other gent, the one you called Lester. Maybe you know where to collar him later on when the time comes. That right?"

"That's the way I figure it."

Relieved, Rutger eased himself back in his saddle. He kept on chewing his tobacco but, urging his horse after Longarm, he killed no more vegetation as they continued across the high, rocky trail they had been following.

They reached Celestial City after nightfall. Shaking off the memories that flooded over him as he entered the town, Longarm rode into a narrow back alley paralleling the main street. He and Rutger rode very slowly, doing their best not to alarm Bat and warn him of their entry —when both men found themselves surrounded not by train robbers, but by Chinese.

They were dressed in their native costume, conical hats and long black, pajama-like pants and tunics. But it was the crossbows so many carried that riveted Longarm's attention, along with the pistols and the few rifles the rest were packing.

And the fact that not one of them was smiling.

Chapter 6

There seemed to be no leader, so Longarm said nothing. Slowly, carefully, he lifted his leg over the cantle and dismounted. The number of Chinese facing them increased, but all of them together moved back cautiously as Longarm turned to survey them. As he did so, he had difficulty keeping his eyes off the many drawn crossbows still aimed at him and Rutger. Longarm knew that if the slightest pressure were exerted on those triggers, both he and Rutger would be impaled on the murderous bolts, as the fletched shafts were called.

"Get down, Rutger," Longarm told his deputy. "Just do it slow-like, so they know we ain't about to attack them."

"I got the idea," Rutger replied.

An older Chinese male hurried through the ranks of the Chinese surrounding them and Longarm smiled in sudden relief. It was his old friend, the tailor Chou Li-Fan. He had aged considerably in the time since Long-arm last saw him. Little was left of the soft, feathery tuft of white hair that adorned his chin. He was more stooped and his elfin, puckered face was a maze of wrinkles. But the eyes were the same—as alert and in-telligent as before.

He clasped both hands before him and bowed twice, his ancient face wreathed in smiles. He was obviously very glad to see Longarm.

"This miserable tailor greets the Most Honorable Knight of the Road once more! Welcome to Celestial City."

"Thanks, Chou," Longarm replied. "Meet my fellow knight, Bob Rutger."

Turning to Rutger, Chou Li-Fan bowed.

"Now would you please tell your friends to lower them crossbows and see to our horses?"

Chou spun about and spoke swiftly, sharply, his sing-song dialect recalling to Longarm many pleasant and many not-so-pleasant memories. Chou's commands were obeyed immediately. Every crossbow was lowered and men sprang forward to take their horses.

"Come," Chou Li-Fan said. "I will show you to my shop and we will talk of your most favorable return."

"You got coffee?" Rutger asked Chou.

"No, but have very strong tea."

"Guess that'll have to do." Rutger sighed wearily.

"Shut up and count your blessings," growled Long-arm. "It's a damn sight better than one of them bolts in your gut."

"Reckon so," Rutger nodded, and said nothing more as he followed after Chou Li-Fan and Longarm through a small back door into the kitchen behind the tailor's shop.

An ancient white-haired Chinese lady, evidently Chou Li-Fan's wife, entered the kitchen. Chou spoke to her softly. Her head a halo of white hair, her back bent permanently, the woman scurried swiftly about the tiny kitchen. Almost at once, it seemed, the stove was lit and steam was pouring from the spout of a silver teapot. With swift, birdlike movements the old woman took down from a cupboard a platter of sweet little cakes festooned with raisins and nuts and set them down in the center of the table. The tea she poured into large pewter mugs and placed them down before each man, her head bent as if she were making an offering to the gods, after which she vanished from the kitchen, leaving it to the men.

"You did not have a wife the last time I was here," Longarm commented as he sipped the powerful tea and hoped there would be more to eat than the small cakes.

"It is a long story," the old tailor said, with more than a hint of weariness in his voice.

"I'd like to hear it. After all, you were supposed to be back in China by this time."

"Ah, yes. Such plans. This miserable tailor remembers them all."

"What happened?"

"We arrived in San Francisco safely enough, but the Ong Leong tong was too powerful. In the streets and back alleys of that accursed city we fought their men bravely enough. But in the end we were forced to compromise."

"Compromise?"

"It was agreed that some would go on to China. The

99

rest would have to return here and continue to mine the jade."

"What'd you do, draw straws to see which of you returned?"

"No. We sent the younger ones home to their ancestral land and the rest pronounced themselves too feeble to make such a tedious journey and returned here. There was one concession only from the Ong Leong chief."

"And what was that?"

"Henceforth our own men would sit in council with the Ong Leong—and for this concession we were obliged to take back here with us those faithless women no longer wanted by the Ong Leong tong."

"You mean that woman who was just in here—your wife . . . ?"

"To the everlasting shame of my first and most virtuous wife, yes. She was one of those who returned with us. For many years she run parlor house in San Francisco. It is frequented by white seamen and is famous throughout the Pacific for its erotic splendor and the unbridled lascivity of its women. I have been most fortunate, however. This woman had no disease and is a most faithful wife and servant. It has not gone so well for many others who returned with me, however."

"Is Ling Chan back here as well?"

"Ling Chan has gone to join his ancestors. He met his end in an alley in San Francisco, with the hatchet of an Ong Leong henchman in his back."

Longarm winced. "What about Sanchez?"

Chou Li-Fan brightened. "He and my daughter Ti-Ling are safely in China. As are many who fought so bravely by your side. And so too are Tai Wong and Wan San." The old tailor almost smiled as he continued.

100

"They have returned to the land of our ancestors, sailed past the Dragon's Eye and into the Tiger's Mouth. As you had hoped, Longarm, they have returned to the Pearl River delta." The old man sighed. "It is enough for those of us who have remained to know this. After all, our unworthy lives are nearly at an end, while those of our children are just beginning."

Longarm munched thoughtfully on one of the cakes and sipped the strong, hot tea. Sanchez had stood by Longarm during some wild times, times when Longarm had found himself caught literally between a rock and a hard place.

"Well, I'm glad to hear about your daughter and Sanchez. But I wish Ling Chan could have made it."

"Now tell me, honorable knight—what brings you to the Celestial City once again?"

"Same thing as before."

"You chase evil men."

"Yes."

"We have many here," Chou sighed. "The Celestial City is getting very crowded."

"I'm looking for a gent and his woman. They might've rode in here a few days ago, leading a long string of pack horses."

The old tailor's eyes gleamed. "And what might those pack horses be packing?"

"A fortune in gold bars."

"And how did these fugitives acquire such wealth?"

"They robbed a train."

"I see."

"I'm after the gold as much as the man and the woman."

"The woman, also?"

101

"She's as dangerous as a scorpion. I want her, too."

"This gold. Who were its original owners?"

Longarm considered a moment. "I guess it would have to be the stockholders of the Link Mine, outside Red Cliff."

Chou's benevolent countenance lost all its benevolence. "The Link Mine?"

"Yes."

Chou pushed himself away from the table and peered cautiously at Longarm. "What you say troubles me. The Link Mine belongs to those who have long exploited and enslaved Chinese laborers. We here in Celestial City have sworn to do all we could to bring down the hateful owners of that enterprise. And the Ong Leong has joined us in that resolve."

"Seems to me the Ong Leong was not all that scrupulous in the days of Dr. Fell."

"As I say before, things are different now. Many of our people are members of the Ong Leong tong, and we have made our feelings felt in the tong's councils."

"I see."

Longarm leaned back and sipped the tea. Through all this Rutger had remained perfectly silent, munching away on the cakes and sipping the tea. But he was not missing a thing, Longarm felt.

Chou smiled and tipped his head slightly. "You say you want just the man and his woman who steal this gold?"

"That's right."

"Is it not strange that one man and his woman could do such a thing as rob a train?"

"They weren't alone when they robbed it. The gang's been whittled down some since."

"Whittled down?"

"It's an expression. Three of the gang members died since they stopped the train and robbed it."

"Died?" Chou's expression lightened slightly. "Do you not mean this most illustrious knight killed them?"

Longarm shrugged. "I had no choice. Anyway, the only ones left now are the gang leader and his woman."

Chou sat back in his chair and regarded Longarm through lidded eyes. Though he had not yet admitted to the presence in Celestial City of Bat and Consuela, it was obvious from Chou's questions and manner that they were here. Now all Longarm had to do was have Chou admit it.

"Well?" Longarm prodded gently. "Are those two here?"

"Yes. We have seen them. They are here."

"When did they arrive?"

"Yesterday. Late in the afternoon."

"Where are they holed up?"

"In the saloon." Chou Li-Fan smiled. "If you will remember, it is the same place where you held your war councils with Ling Chang and the makers of the crossbows."

"I remember."

"But I am afraid the two you seek are not alone."

"What do you mean?"

"Long before they arrived, for two months now, a pack of evil horsemen entered our city. At first we made them welcome, hoping they would slake their thirst and ride on. Instead, they began to pillage our little city at will, and soon made the saloon their home. And now they have joined forces with those two train robbers you seek."

103

Longarm frowned. These other men could not have been waiting here for Bat. If they had been accomplices, Bat would have mentioned them. No, it was just rotten luck. They just happened to be here when Bat arrived.

"These others," Longarm asked Chou, "how have they survived? What are they living on?"

"They have robbed and pillaged two of our food stores, and taken meat at will from our smoke shops."

"Do you have any idea who they might be?"

"No, we do not. We have tried to drive them out, but they have killed many of our people. Only our crossbows and old pistols and rifles have kept them at bay. It is a game they seem to like. I think they would prefer to stay here and make this their permanent nest once they have cleaned us out."

"How many are there?"

"Four."

"Only four?"

"They have many guns. And rifles. And they know how to use them." Chou smiled. "But now you and your tall companion have arrived. When the time comes, you will lead us against these vermin. Is that not so?"

"What's wrong with right now?"

"The Ong Leong has been made aware of our predicament and why it is we have been forced to stop mining jade. They have promised to send men to help us destroy this nest. It would be preferable for you to wait and join forces with them."

"I don't think I'll wait for them, Chou."

Chou shrugged. "But why not? They will be here soon. Speak with them. There are many in the Ong Leong who remember your efforts on our behalf."

104

"I could be waiting for a long, long time. My deputy here and I don't have all that much time." Longarm turned to Rutger. "That right, Rutger?"

His mouth full of cake, Rutger nodded quickly.

Chou smiled placatingly. "But nothing this vital can be settled over tea and these miserable cakes. Later, perhaps, you may be persuaded to see things our way." He got quickly to his feet. "I will see now to quarters for you and your illustrious deputy."

"What the hell's he mean by that?" Rutger demanded as he wolfed down the last raisin cake. "It'll be a cool day in hell before we let him talk us into seeing things their way. Like you said, we could be holed up here forever waiting for them other chinks to get here all the way from San Francisco. Besides, what in the hell do we need them for?"

Longarm glanced at him. He didn't like the tone of Rutger's remark, not one bit. He said coldly, "I got two things to tell you, Rutger. The first is I don't want to hear you refer to these people as chinks. And the second thing is, I'm in charge here. If you don't like it you can ride back to where you came from. That clear?"

"Jesus, don't be so touchy."

"Is that clear, I said."

"It's clear."

"Good."

"What's this about him calling you Longarm? And a battle you and his people was in? Sounds like a war."

"It was damn close to it. When I have time, I'll fill you in."

Chou Li-Fan hurried back into the kitchen, pleased, his hands clasped before him. "Not far from here is a safe house. There both of you will find a hot tub and a

105

clean bed. We will speak again in the morning."

"Sure," said Longarm, getting to his feet, "but do you mind tellin' me when you're expecting this contingent of Ong Leong fighters from San Francisco?"

"I am sorry. I cannot tell you that."

"That does it, Chou. We can't wait. We have to move quick. I'm sure you understand."

The tailor bowed from the waist. "Will the most honorable Knight of the Road honor me by waiting until tomorrow for further discussions on this matter?"

"Are you the one in charge of things here now?" Longarm asked.

Chou nodded humbly. "Alas, yes. It has fallen upon my unworthy shoulders, the task of keeping order in this most disorderly of all lands."

"I'm tired," said Rutger. "Where's that washtub you mentioned—and the bed."

A Chinese in his early forties stepped through the door. He seemed fit enough and his alert eyes watched the two men narrowly.

"Here is Tan San," Chou said. "He will lead you to your quarters for the night. Sleep well."

His hands tucked into his ample sleeves, Chou Li-Fan bowed formally. The discussion was obviously at an end.

With a shrug, Longarm followed Tan San out into the alley. The two men had not taken more than half a dozen steps with their escort when something like a sap came down hard on the back of his head. As darkness fogged his senses, he heard Rutger's grunts as the man struggled with his attackers. Then came the sound of Rutger hitting the alley floor. And that was all Longarm remembered as his knees turned to water and another

106

blow to his head sent him reeling into darkness.

When Longarm regained consciousness, he found himself lying stark naked on a leather-cushioned sofa of some kind, as clean as a plucked chicken, and with a pounding in his head that set his teeth on edge. A lovely dark-eyed, dark-haired girl of twenty or so was leaning anxiously over him as she laved his long body with a warm sponge. She worked intently, eagerly, as if this action would be enough to rid him of his murderous headache. Unfortunately, it wasn't.

He groaned and put his hand to his head, even though he knew it would do no good. A tiny horde of demons was blasting a tunnel through his head from one ear to the other.

"They hit you too hard," the girl said, shaking her head in concern.

"If they had hit me any harder, they would have buried me," Longarm told her fiercely, his anger building rapidly.

"We are so sorry."

Longarm looked at her through pain-narrowed eyes. "You really did say that, did you?"

She pulled back and nodded, wringing out her sponge over the pan of hot water she had been dipping it into. She was wearing a tight-fitting blouse and a skirt equally tight-fitting, both of a subtle shade of jade green. Her earrings were of jade, as was the comb that held her tightly bound hair in place on the top of her head. Her cheekbones gleamed duskily, her eyes glowed, and when she spoke, he could see teeth like pearls. About her hung a subtle fragrance. He was glad he no longer stank of horse and sweat.

"Just wanted to be sure," he told her, amused despite

himself. "Now, what've you got for this granddaddy of all headaches your friends gave me?"

"I have something for you to drink."

"You sure it'll help?"

"Yes, but it will make you drowsy."

"So what."

She shrugged. "I would not waⁱt you to get too drowsy." She glanced down at him, her dark eyes glowing with excitement. He followed her bold gaze and was astonished to see the small tree growing out of his crotch.

"Never mind that," he growled, "just fix this headache. I'll drink cow piss if it'll do the job."

She dropped the sponge into the bowl and fled from the room as silently as a moonbeam. Longarm swung his feet off the couch and rested them on the floor. It was thickly carpeted, warm to his touch. At that moment he didn't like having to use his eyes for anything important, but what he saw of the room impressed him. Its walls were covered with thickly brocaded drapes that were in turn covered with exquisitely woven scenes from China, the one directly across from him portraying snow-capped mountain peaks in China, with great rolling clouds of mist drifting up from the valleys below, some of them almost obscuring the mountain peaks.

His couch was set against one wall, and facing him were two chairs in the far corners of the room. A small table with a black lacquered top sat in the middle of the room and to his right he saw a large bed sitting on a pedestal. The silken covers were already turned back for him and gleamed seductively in the flickering light of the candle that sat on a small night stand.

The girl returned with a cup.

"What's your name?" he asked, reaching for it.

"Lei Nin."

"What's it mean?"

"Moon shower."

He drank the potion she had handed him in one swift gulp. It had a slightly musty taste and for a moment he thought for some crazy reason of bats' wings and did not think his stomach was going to let it stay down, but as soon as he leaned back once again on the couch, the faint nausea passed. Lei Nin had been correct. Almost immediately he felt drowsy and for a moment thought he was actually going to pitch headlong off the couch.

He felt Lei Nin helping him up off the couch and over to the bed. He slapped face down onto the cool silken sheets, then rolled over. The headache was fading fast, but so were his perceptions. The ceiling spun crazily—or was it the bed? He clung to it as he grinned crazily up at Lei Nin. In bed with him, she closed her fiery lips over his and held on tenaciously, letting their fire build another fire deep in Longarm's groin.

"You are taking advantage of me," he protested feebly.

"I know that," she said, then kissed him harder, her tongue probing deeply, her hot hand closing about his raging erection.

"What in hell're you doin' in this place? I thought only old people lived here."

She laughed, took a small bite out of his ear, and then moved her lips down his hairy chest. "Now you know why I am so eager to comfort you."

He felt her slipping over onto him. In a moment she was astride him, and his erection slipped into her warm moistness, plunging deep. She leaned back and, grabbing both his hands, began to ride him. His headache was still there, but only as a distant memory. As he felt himself building to a roaring climax, he realized he was cured of his headache.

Sighing, he leaned back and let it happen. He would find out what this was all about the next day. Meanwhile, he had a night to get through.

He had gotten through the night somehow and it was dawn. He was wide awake. His headache was gone. A clean shaft of sunlight was streaming in the window, gleaming dust motes dancing in it. Through the break in the curtains he could see one of the towering peaks that hemmed in this narrow valley. And Lei Nin was fastened to him, her arms about his thigh.

This was what had awakened him. Reaching down, he took her by the shoulders and pulled her up to him.

"I have not finished."

"I don't want to finish that way," he said roughly, pulling her over, then shifting swiftly up onto her.

"Ah," she cried, spreading her legs eagerly. He plunged in quickly so as not to cool himself off any and felt her long thighs closing tightly about his waist. He lifted a little and swung one of her legs in under him, allowing her to close the leg tightly. Then he did the same to her other leg. With both legs closed tightly, she had his engorged member in as tight a clasp as he could remember. She loved it and squeezed him hungrily as he began to pound away.

"This is better," he muttered to her. "I like to give as much as I get."

"You are so generous," she muttered through clamped teeth, meeting him thrust for thrust.

110

There was no more conversation after that. Holding off as long as he could, Longarm was pleased at last to feel Lei Nin shuddering out of control beneath him as she came in a series of wild paroxysms, her teeth still clenched, her face rigid. With an explosive cry of release, she collapsed back down upon the bed and let Longarm ease out of her.

"Yes," she sighed. "That was much nicer. But you slept so soundly, I could not think of a better way to arouse you."

"You exhausted me last night. I think you are insatiable."

"All women are insatiable."

"I admit, it sure as hell beats an alarm clock."

"Yes," she murmured dreamily, reaching up to run her fingers through his thick shock of hair. "I am sure it does. Maybe some morning you wake me up like that. Mmm. You are so dark. I think perhaps you Indian at first. But the eyes, they are not the eyes of Indian."

"What do you know of Indians?"

"I know," she said. "Last winter they come down to this village for food, when it is cold and they can find no deer to kill. These are renegades, I think. They are far from their reservation."

Longarm nodded. Utes, maybe. There were a lot out here in the mountains still as determined as ever not to be put on a federal tether. And more power to them.

There had been little chance for conversation the night before and Longarm had been unable to learn anything from Lei Nin concerning the attack on him and Rutger. He did not know if they were prisoners or not. If they were, they were certainly being kept better than most prisoners. He had thought he could trust Chou Li-

111

Fan, and it pained him to realize that he could not be trusted, after all.

Longarm propped himself up on his elbow. "All right, Lei Nin, what's going on?"

"Why, as you can see, we are resting before breakfast," she replied, smiling impishly. Snuggling closer, she threw one leg up onto him, her knee nudging his crotch gently. Then she began to blow on one earlobe with her hot, perfumed breath. "Shall we have another before we eat?"

"Can't do it, Lei Nin. Too weak. I need nourishment. Now answer me. Why was I attacked after I left Chou Li-Fan's last night and thrown into this silk-lined prison with you?"

"Yes," she said, pulling back and gazing down at him. "I am your jailer. It is true."

"What is going on?"

She shrugged. "All I know is they bring you to me last night and tell me to take care of you. You need a bath, so I bathe you. Then you wake up and I see what else you need, so I take care of that, too. There is nothing else I can tell you."

"What about you, then? You speak damned good English compared to the others."

"Since I come to this country as little girl, I speak English. I have work in many houses to please men. Many books I have read. I cannot be on my back all the time, you see? So I ask questions and refuse certain men because of what they want me to do. That is why the Ong Leong send me here to comfort the old men. But they are beyond such comfort, poor devils. All I do is drive them wild." She sighed. "Now you know all about me."

112

"What's Chou Li-Fan up to?"

"I tell you, I do not know. I am, like you, a prisoner in the Celestial City. I do as I am told."

Longarm got up, wrapped one of the silken bedsheets about his tall frame, and walked over to the door. He tried the knob, but the door was locked. He rattled it and would have kicked it, but he was barefooted. He turned then to gaze back across the room at Lei Nin.

"You left this room last night to get that medicine. The door was not locked then. That much I remember."

She sighed. "I know. But it is now."

"Then you are not lying. You're a prisoner, too."

She laughed. "What does it matter? Do not worry. Soon they will bring us breakfast. We are safe."

"I'm not so sure. Where are my clothes?"

"They are being laundered. When they are dry, they will be ironed and brought back here." She smiled archly. "Until then, you have no clothes to wear. So you see, it is foolish for you to worry. After all, what can a naked man do?"

He was about to show her when a little Chinese lady was let into the room and a breakfast fit for royalty— Chinese royalty—was wheeled in on a little table. The aroma that came from under the domed silver covers placed over the hot plates had his stomach roiling eagerly. His jaws ached. He had never been this hungry in his life before, it seemed. With a sigh, he sat in one of the chairs and allowed himself to be served.

He would show Lei Nin what a naked man could do later.

Chapter 7

By the third morning, Longarm was restless enough to consider making a break for it as soon as the little Chinese lady brought them their breakfast. Lei Nin was finally asleep in a tangle of bedclothes, her long, coal-black tresses sprawled gleaming across the silk sheets. Longarm had won the first round, maybe, but he had never before had to contend with a woman as insatiable as Lei Nin, and the prospect of attempting to outlast her for another day did not please him. The irony of this was not lost on him. It seemed that as soon as a man got what he claimed he always wanted, he found he didn't really want it after all. He grinned with some affection down at Lei Nin's sprawled form. Not all at once, anyway.

But getting worn down to a nubbin in the arms of a woman was the least of Longarm's worries. He was a prisoner in the Celestial City and the object of his mission was tantalizingly close—only a few blocks away—with a gold shipment Longarm had telegraphed Billy Vail he would not return without regaining.

He was pacing in front of the window, his bedsheet flung over his tall frame, toga-like, when the door swung open. Instead of the little old woman, three surprisingly tall Chinese gentlemen stepped into the room. They were dressed in the traditional black tunics and trousers of their fellow countrymen, but they had abandoned the conical hats for black Stetsons and their baggy trousers were tucked into highly polished black riding boots.

The tallest one stepped forward. He was a handsome, cold-eyed oriental with eyes of obsidian, but Longarm thought he detected a hint of amusement in their cold, fathomless depths as he took in Longarm's ridiculous situation.

"I am Tom Shan," he said. "And you must be the Honorable Knight of the Road, the famous Longarm."

"I don't know how honorable I am."

"You admit to being famous, then."

"My mother didn't raise a son foolish enough to admit to anything."

"But it is known throughout the Ong Leong that it was you who killed the infamous Dr. Fell and his equally dishonorable daughter. Is this not true, then?"

"That's a long story. You'll need a few more details to get it all straight. But right now, I want my clothes. Then I want to know why I am a prisoner of the Ong Leong."

Tom Shan spoke to one of his men, who promptly vanished out the door. "Your cleaned and freshly ironed

116

clothes will be brought to you." He smiled apologetically. "But not that clever vest of yours with the watch and the derringer. And not your holster with its most deadly .44 Colt."

"In that case, I'll still feel pretty naked."

"But you must relax, Longarm. You are among friends."

"Yeah. Some friends. They give you little cakes, then they bury a sledgehammer in your skull."

"And throw you in this miserable cell," Tom Shan finished ironically, "with only this beautiful and accomplished courtesan to keep you warm."

As Tom Shan said this, Lei Nin shook herself awake and, stretching herself like a cat, sat up in the bed. Only when she saw all four men gazing at her dusky nakedness did she think to pull a sheet up over her small, pert breasts. With an impish smile, she took in what was going on and scooted back against the headboard to watch and listen.

Tom Shan turned his attention back to Longarm. "Rendering you unconscious, I am afraid, was the only way Chou Li-Fan knew to disarm you and your companion."

"How's my deputy? You fellows weren't very gentle, you know. We're lucky our heads are still on our shoulders."

"Your deputy is in another room. He has suffered as you have, I understand. Poor man."

"I came as a friend, Tom Shan. Why did Chou Li-Fan think he had to attack us like that?"

"Alas, the old man is not all that wise in the ways of violence. He simply wanted to make sure you did not move too soon on that gold shipment. As he pointed out

117

to you, it is the property of men with whom the Ong Leong has a score to settle. He wanted to hold you in check until we arrived from San Francisco."

"From the local chapter of the Ong Leong."

Tom Shan acknowledged this with a quick nod. "We rode in this morning and heard about your capture. We came at once."

"Thanks. I'm still waiting for my clothes, by the way."

Tom Shan paused for a moment, then said, "There is one detail. Chou Li-Fan found dynamite in your saddle-bags."

Longarm shrugged. "That's where I kept it, all right."

"There were no blasting caps. How do you detonate the dynamite?"

"A bullet is as good a way as any."

Tom Shan nodded. "This is what I thought. Now, one more question. Will the most famous and honorable Longarm help us rid ourselves of these hateful gunmen who have already killed so many of our people?"

"Sure. But only if you let Bat Coulter and his woman go back with me along with the gold."

Tom Shan smiled. "Have a fine breakfast. Then you and your deputy will help us root out these insects who have infested the Celestial City. Is it agreed?"

"What you mean is, first things first."

Tom Shan smiled and bowed slightly. "Yes."

Longarm was in no position to bargain. He shrugged. "Agreed."

Tom Shan and his companions left the room. A moment later Longarm's breakfast arrived, and soon after, his clothes, laundered and neatly pressed. As Tom Shan had promised, his vest with the derringer and his .44 were missing.

He was supposed to help Tom Shan and his Ong Leong warriors from San Francisco rid the Celestial City of its unwelcome visitors without firing a shot, it appeared.

Nate Heller was stationed at the saloon window. Peering through the gathering dusk, he said, "There's more of these damned chinks every minute. All day I been watchin' 'em. They're like cockroaches coming out of a wall."

"Yeah. I been noticing," Kroner said, throwing down his hand. He scraped back his chair, got to his feet, and walked over to the window. As he came to a halt beside Heller, he said, "I think maybe we might've worn out our welcome."

From the table, Bim chuckled and began to deal himself a hand of solitaire. It was a soft, mean chuckle. "I wonder why."

Hank Fletcher was on the second floor. His hands grasping the balcony railing, he peered down at them. "I been watching from the window up here," he called down. "There's something up, all right."

Kroner glanced up at him. "What can you see?"

"From all over they're moving closer, ducking from alley to alley, keeping hid all the while, or tryin' to."

"If you saw them, they ain't keepin' hid."

"All I see's a hat here, a running figure there. They're stayin' hid as best they can, but they're movin' closer all the time. We better be careful. Something's up."

Kroner peered back out the window and spoke mus-

119

ingly to Heller. "If they try to rush us, we'll cut them down like we been doin'—but maybe it's time we pulled out."

"Where to?"

"That hideout of Bat's. Lost Eagle Pass."

"Think you can find it?"

"If he can't, I can," said Consuela from the stairs. She had combed out her long hair and let it flow down her back. The long tresses gleamed like the sky at midnight. Her appearance stirred every man there clear to his boot straps. Kroner had been keeping her all to himself, and at that moment every man there hated Kroner very much.

"You been there before?" Kroner asked her.

"With Bat. When we were getting ready for the raise."

"It's south of here, as I remember."

"That's right. Southwest, to be exact."

"That settles it. Help us load up the pack horses, Consuela. We're moving out of here tonight."

"Then we better start now," she said. "Only I ain't lifting that gold myself. All I'm doing is checking out the aparejos, make sure they don't shift any if we have to move out fast."

Kroner grinned approvingly at her. Then he looked around at his men. "Looks like we got ourselves quite a woman here," he said. "She's gonna be a real help."

Grudgingly, they nodded.

"So I don't want none of you givin' her trouble, see? Nate, Hank, Bim, get on out back now and start loading the gold. I'll stay here at the window an' keep an eye out."

With Consuela in the lead, Nate and Hank walked to

120

the rear of the saloon and stepped out into the back alley. Bim, still seated at the table, swept up the cards he had been studying and got to his feet.

"Don't strain yourself, Pete," he said, chuckling, and moved off after the others.

Kroner didn't like Bim's remark, but he knew enough to let it pass. He'd take care of the son of a bitch later, once they were out of this crazy town and that incredible treasure was his—and his alone.

He saw a dark-clad figure packing a rifle dart across a narrow alley and duck into a feed store across the street. Then another followed. And still another. Hell, that damn feed store was probably crawling with them by this time. A grim smile on his face, he unlimbered his Colt and pushed himself through the batwings. Striding boldly out onto the porch, he lifted his revolver and sent a round through one of the feed store's windows. The great pane shattered and collapsed noisily. Then he fired through the adjoining window, and kept on firing until not a single window in the storefront remained intact.

Smiling broadly, he turned and headed back into the saloon. As he pushed through the batwings, a sudden fusillade of rifle fire shattered the door, sending shards of wood clear across the room. Ducking swiftly out of the line of fire, Kroner flattened himself against the wall, then peered cautiously out the window. The Chinese had left the feed store and were out on its porch, hunched down behind flour and pickle barrels. Some of them, Kroner noted, were wearing Stetsons. Damn. They must have brought in help of some kind.

Consuela appeared. "Trouble, Pete. Most gold loaded now, but three horses, they can't go nowheres."

"Damn it! What's wrong with them?"

"Two is lame, the other one, he is weak like kitten. I think he have the distemper."

"Shit, he might already've given it to the others."

Consuela shrugged. "Maybe so. Bat, he work them too hard to get here. Now we do not have enough to carry all the gold."

"Sure we do. Double up the loads."

Consuela shook her head firmly. "No, Pete. That will make it too heavy for them. Soon these horses, too, will be lame. Then we lose everything."

"Damn it, Consuela! We can't leave any of that gold here!"

She thought a moment. "Listen, Pete. Maybe the horses take gold only a little way from here. Then maybe we stop and bury what gold we cannot take and come back for it later. What you think?"

Kroner left the window to join Consuela. She was right. He should have thought of that himself. Get it the hell out of this place first, then bury it somewhere. There was no other way.

He had almost reached Consuela when they both heard something skitter up onto the porch and slam into the side of the building. Kroner paused, wondering what it was. A second later came the crack of a rifle and the entire front wall of the saloon disappeared in a blinding flash, sending him and Consuela hurtling through the back door.

"Dynamite!" Kroner cried, scrambling to his feet. "So that's the way them bastards want to play, is it?" He turned to a gaping Nate Heller. "Where's that box of dynamite we took from that other one? I said it might come in handy!"

122

A dazed Consuela picked herself up off the alley. "It's over here," she said, rubbing the dust out of her eyes and throwing her long hair back. "I already packed it."

A second charge of dynamite detonated in the alley beside the saloon, sending a sheet of flame up the outside wall. Grimly determined to give his attackers a dose of their own medicine, Kroner hurried after Consuela, yelling to Heller and the others to join him.

"One more stick should do it," Rutger said to Longarm.

"Go ahead, then. Throw it."

Inside the feed store, Rutger stood up and heaved the stick of dynamite out through one of its shattered windows. Longarm watched the stick hit, roll, then come to rest against the wall of the building next to the saloon. Lifting the Winchester to his shoulder, he aimed quickly and fired. He missed. Compressing his lips grimly, he aimed more carefully and fired again at the dynamite. The bullet hit home. The dynamite blossomed, its fearsome detonation sending great tongues of flame high into the air between the two buildings.

From down the street came a high, piercing shout. Longarm recognized Tom Shan's voice. His high, sing-song cry Longarm assumed was the equivalent of "Let's go, men! Get 'em now!" A second later Longarm saw Tom Shan dashing down the street toward the blazing saloon, a horde of Chinese at his heels.

They carried weapons of all sorts: crossbows, old flintlocks, pistols. But they were not firing them. Instead they were waving them and shouting at the top of their lungs, as if their screeching alone might send the hated interlopers out of their city. A second band swept up the street from the other direction, led by Tom Shan's friends. Longarm got to his feet to watch when he saw something fall into the midst of the Chinese. At once they lost heart, their charge on the saloon disintegrating. Like ants fleeing a trampling foot, they scrambled back the way they had come. Then a shot came from the roof of the building next to the saloon and a sudden, devastating explosion erupted in their midst.

Mangled bodies went flying. Those Chinese who were not flattened by the blast crawled and dragged their torn bodies back up the street as fast as they could. Then another stick of dynamite landed in the street, this one skittering toward the feed store. Longarm heard it slap against a porch post.

"Down!" he cried, his right arm slapping Rutger to the floor beside him.

A short burst of rifle fire from across the street detonated the stick. The blast was enough to deafen Longarm momentarily. Shards of glass, wood and plaster whistled over his head. He waited until the air was clear before looking up, and as he squinted through smoke and flames, he glimpsed one of Bat's gang peering around a corner of the building next to the saloon.

The son of a bitch was holding a stick of dynamite.

Longarm brought up his rifle and snapped off a shot. The fellow disappeared in a titanic blast that took off a corner of the building he had been leaning against. Rutger shook his head in amazement at the shot. But there was no time for comment as another stick of dynamite tumbled across the street toward them. Another short rattle of gunfire came after it, triggering a blast that thoroughly demolished the feed store.

By that time Longarm and Rutger had already flung

themselves into the alley behind it. Shielding his face from the sudden blaze, Longarm saw that Rutger had had the presence of mind to snatch up his last four sticks of dynamite.

He grinned at Rutger. "You keep standing around with those in your hands and you're liable to blow us both to hell and back."

"You want me to toss them back into that blazing shop?"

"Just find a safe spot for them."

As Rutger nodded and headed for an abandoned house up a side alley, Longarm saw Chou Li-Fan running down the alley toward him, his face distraught. Longarm was afraid the old man would have a heart attack before he reached him.

"Honorable Longarm!" Chou Li-Fan cried. "You must hurry!"

"What's wrong?"

Chou pulled up in front of him. "You must hurry!" he repeated. "It is Tom Shan. He is in the street. He hurt bad! Soon more dynamite will kill him!"

Longarm left Chou behind, found a clear alley leading to the main street, and darted out into it. He slipped past fearfully maimed Chinese and headed for the front of the blazing saloon. It was close to dark by now, but the burning buildings on both sides of the street enabled Longarm to pick out Tom Shan and the two men he had brought with him lying face down in the middle of the street.

As Longarm neared Tom Shan, he saw that both his comrades were dead or close to it. Their vital parts were shattered so completely they looked like oversized rag dolls and both of them lay in darkening pools of blood.

But Tom Shan, though obviously wounded, was still conscious.

He raised his head as Longarm knelt beside him. "It is my right leg, Longarm," he gasped. "I can move it, but I can put no weight on it."

"Any other wounds?"

"No. This time I am lucky."

Something hit the ground behind Longarm. He turned. Rolling toward him was another stick of dynamite. He grabbed for it, missed, then caught it from behind. As he stood up to throw it back, a sudden fusillade of bullets sang past his head like angry hornets.

"Throw it, you fool!" gasped Tom Shan.

"I'm looking for a target."

Tom Shan ducked his head and covered it with both arms. Then Longarm saw one of the outlaws step out from the alley beside the blazing saloon and lift a rifle to his shoulder. Heaving the dynamite, Longarm watched it vanish into the blazing saloon. A second later the saloon went up in a final titanic blast, and the rifleman vanished into a flaming vortex of smoke and debris that whisked him straight to hell.

Longarm bent, flung Tom Shan over his shoulder, and raced back up the street and into cover. As Chou Li-Fan and others crowded around to see to the wounded man, Longarm heard the rapid beat of hooves thundering across the wooden bridge outside of town.

At that moment Rutger ran up. "You hear that?"

"I hear it."

Bat and his men were making a break for it. It had been a costly victory for the Ong Leong and their Chinese clients, but they had finally rid themselves of the gang of interlopers who had nested for so long in their

126

midst and halted that precious flow of jade to China. And there was little doubt that Bat Coulter and his cohorts would never again return to the Celestial City.

Unfortunately, with Bat Coulter on the run, with him went the gold shipment.

Chapter 8

A piece was gone from the calf of Tom Shan's leg. Outside of that, as he had said, he was lucky. Once the wound was bound and the bleeding stopped, he met with Longarm and Bob Rutger in Chou Li-Fan's kitchen. Leaning his makeshift crutch against the nearby wall, he sat down at the kitchen table beside Chou Li-Fan and reached for the mug of tea that had been set before his place.

"They had dynamite too," Tom Shan said, eyeing Longarm unhappily.

"I should have thought of that," Longarm admitted.

"Then you knew they had it?"

"The one who handled the dynamite for Bat's gang was gone. Rutger and I saw him leaving Celestial City. I assumed he had taken the dynamite with him."

"But he didn't."

"That's what it looks like."

"Still, they are gone now. We suffered losses, but the jade production will resume tomorrow."

"Your job is done."

"So it seems."

"I'm sorry about your two buddies."

"So am I—and the many others who were killed. Thank you for saving my unworthy life."

"Glad I could help."

"You are either very lucky or very brave."

Longarm shrugged.

"What are your plans now?"

"To get after Bat and that gold."

Tom Shan sighed. "While the gold was within the Celestial City, the Ong Leong had some claim to it. But no longer. Go after it, then. When will you leave?"

"First thing tomorrow, if we can get our firepower back."

Tom Shan glanced at Chou Li-Fan. The old man spoke up. "The order has already been given," he told Longarm. "Your weapons will be returned to you along with your mounts. They have been grained and well rested. You should make good time."

"Do you have any idea where this gang is heading?" Tom Shan asked.

"Bob says there's a pass southwest of here. We figure they'll have to take that if they want to get out of this basin."

Tom Shan nodded, finished his tea, and got painfully to his feet. "I go now to see to the wounded. These are old men, Longarm. They will not heal as quickly as you or I."

Using his crutch, Tom Shan left the kitchen. Chou Li-Fan got up also, bowing. "I go with Tom Shan," he told them.

Longarm finished his tea and stood up also. He and Rutger were being rushed, but Longarm didn't mind. Not if Lei Nin was still waiting for him up in that lovely cell where he had been incarcerated for so long. The only thing was, he doubted if she would give him much chance to sleep.

But what did that matter? He could always sleep on the trail.

Pete Kroner, Nate Heller, and Consuela made at best ten miles that night. When dawn broke over the mountain ridges hemming them in, it was clear that they would have to find a place fast where they could unload and bury at least three-quarters of the gold. The horses were already stumbling, their tails dragging, their heads low, and already the aparejos had shifted dangerously on two of the horses.

"Hey, Pete," said Nate Heller, pointing. "How about up there in that cave."

"Where, damn it?" Kroner asked, shading his eyes.

"I see it. Yes!" Consuela cried, pointing also. "On that ridge, back in among the rocks."

Kroner saw it also and nodded grimly. "I only hope these horses can make it that far."

"We will go very slow," Consuela told him, dismounting. "We will lead them very careful."

With a weary sigh, Kroner dismounted and followed Consuela's example, and in about an hour they managed to reach the cave entrance. Unloading the horses and lugging the gold into the cave was a tedious, exhausting exercise, and it was not completed until an hour or so before noon.

It was Consuela who thought of going back over their trail and brushing it clean with a pine branch, then following behind them doing the same when they rode out and made for the pass. Watching her, Kroner was pleased. The damned Mex had a head on her shoulders. Maybe he'd keep her.

Nate Heller was watching Consuela, too. It galled him to think of a woman like this coupling with Pete Kroner. She deserved better, and he, Nate Heller, was a damn sight better. In every way. He was cleaner than Pete and younger and a lot more appreciative of a good woman. Nate hated the way Pete treated Consuela, without any real appreciation. Hell, of the two, she was the one doing all the thinking.

Well, he'd bide his time. Once they got through this damn pass and reached that hideout poor Bat had provided.

As Consuela pulled her horse alongside Pete's, he looked over at her. "Where'd you learn that trick, Consuela? You part redskin, are you?"

"Maybe so."

"Hell, you better not be. I ain't no squaw man."

Consuela smiled. "You not like to sleep with Indian? They very good, I hear."

"Damn savages. They stink."

Consuela held her tongue. Why was it, she wondered, that gringos smelled so bad and then blamed everyone else for the stink? She did not like this gringo any more than she had liked Bat Coulter. And when the time came, maybe she would get that fool Nate Heller

132

to help her. She knew what Heller wanted. His eyes could not leave her. She felt them crawling over her like obscene bugs.

It was all the same, she realized. Men were so much stronger than women, but their lusts made them like children, and this time Consuela would win out over them. She had waited a long time for this opportunity. But she knew where that cave was, and it would be she, not Pete Kroner, who came back for those heavy aparejos.

Their loads lightened, the pack horses were able to make good time and four days later, a little before sundown, they reached Lost Eagle Pass. With Pete in the lead, they crossed a stretch of gravel and cut up toward the thin stand of scrub pine that clothed the mountain's flank. Once in the pine, he followed a narrow game trail and came at last to the cabin and outbuildings Bat Coulter had been heading for when he took that fateful turning onto the road that led into Celestial City.

While Nate took care of the horses, Pete collapsed wearily in a large wooden chair and watched Consuela prepare their supper. All they had packed was hardtack, bacon, beans, and coffee, but Bat had thoughtfully stocked the cupboards with canned goods and there were sacks of potatoes, salt, beans, and flour in the bins under the sink. There was even a huge tin of sugar. Meanwhile, the cabin's generous size made it seem luxurious to Kroner after the cramped weeks he had spent in that damned saloon. There were two bedrooms and a large kitchen—living room. A huge stone fireplace dominated one wall. The pump to the well was just outside the back door, and Pete watched contentedly as Consuela lugged in buckets of water.

In preparing the meal she did well, considering that all the pots and pans had to be scrubbed thoroughly, the coffee pot especially. By the time she had placed a meal down before them, Nate had come in from the barn and planted himself down on a cot along one wall. Neither of them offered to help.

At last, wiping a wisp of black hair off her forehead, she glanced over at her lords and masters. "It's ready. Ain't you two goin' to wash up?"

"Hell, what is this?" Kroner cracked, walking over to the table and pulling out a chair. "The Denver House?"

She was too tired to argue the point. They ate silently, the sound of them wolfing down their food filling the large kitchen. When they had swilled down all the coffee, Kroner produced a fifth of whiskey and filled his cup, grinning.

"Well, we made it," he announced.

"We better not show any smoke tomorrow," Consuela said. "That big lawman will be after us."

"You let me worry about him. We got a clear view of the pass. He don't know we're up here. He'll walk into a pasture of hell when he does show up—if he's still after us, that is."

"He ain't that easy to fool."

Kroner had gotten a pretty good look at the jasper they were referring to. He had seen him pick off Bim Sands while the poor son of a bitch was waiting to throw another stick at the feed store. According to Consuela, this tall bastard was someone that a member of Bat's gang had sworn he had killed—only to have him turn up at the train and raise hell with the heist. "Just who the hell is he?" he demanded of Consuela.

"He called himself Jed Morgan. He must be a lawman. Bat let him join the gang, then got suspicious."

"Looks like Bat should've got suspicious *before* he let him join."

"Bat was a fool," she said, getting up to clear off the table.

"Well, you ain't travelin' with a fool this time, Consuela." Grinning, he reached out for her.

She pulled back irritably. "Not now, Pete. I got plenty to do yet. I got to clear off the table and wash the dishes in cold water."

He belched. "I'll be waitin' in the bedroom."

If he had expected her to jump with joy at the prospect, he was sorely disappointed. A load of dishes in her hands, she turned her back on him and walked over to the sink. Taking his bottle with him, Kroner slouched into the bedroom. He found no sheets on the stained mattress, but paid this no heed as he lay back down on it, his boots still on.

He would let Consuela pull them off for him, he decided, reaching for the bottle.

When Consuela looked in on him half an hour later, Pete was asleep with his mouth open, the empty whiskey bottle lying on its side on the floor beside the bed. The lazy bastard had not even bothered to take off his boots, she noted.

She did not enter the bedroom. Instead, she reached in, closed the door softly, then walked to the second bedroom. A candle was flickering on the nightstand beside the bed. Nate was still wide awake. A saddle blanket flung over his naked frame, he had a cigarette in his mouth and was leaning back against the headboard, his arms crossed behind his head. She did not fail to notice

135

his holstered sixgun looped close at hand about the bed-post.

Entering the bedroom, she smiled and sat lightly on the bed beside him. "Build a cigarette for me too, will you, Nate?"

"Sure," he said eagerly, reaching into the night-stand's drawer where he had stashed his fixings. Working swiftly, deftly, he built her a cigarette and lit it for her with a sulfur match. She took a long drag on the cigarette and leaned her head back, her eyes closed, letting the nicotine set her heart to racing as she sucked the smoke deep into her lungs.

"Mmm," she said. "I been wanting a smoke for a long time."

"Didn't know you smoked, Consuela."

She looked at him. "There's a lot you don't know about me, Nate."

"I guess that's right."

"I got hungers and needs like any man."

"Sure. I can understand that."

"I was sorry that first night—I mean, when Pete interrupted us. It must've been tough on you, too." She smiled warmly at him. "I mean, you was sure all set to go."

"I was, that's for damn sure," Nate admitted.

"But now I'm Pete's woman. I do as he says—or else."

"He's the boss," Nate said glumly, his eyes devouring her.

As soon as she had finished the dishes and cleaned off the table, she had washed herself as thoroughly as she could and combed out her hair. Then she had opened the top three buttons on her blouse. She wore no corset and there was nothing under her skirt. She hated

136

petticoats and slips even in this chill climate. She knew that Nate could see the swell of her naked breasts whenever she leaned close to him.

"He doesn't have to be."

Nate swallowed. Tiny beads of perspiration stood out on his forehead. "What do you mean?"

"Don't you know?"

"Hell, Consuela, if I thought for a minute there was any chance that you and I —that maybe we—"

She stopped him in mid-sentence by leaning close and fastening her warm, passionate lips over his. At the same time she rested one hand on his crotch and was not surprised to find an enormous bulge. Reaching under the blanket, her lips still fastened to his, she began to stroke his engorged member.

With a groan, he pulled her to him, his lips working frantically. She hiked up her skirt and pressed against him, her tongue grappling lasciviously with his. Flinging aside the blanket, he rolled frantically over onto her, his knee thrusting up between her thighs to spread her legs. She offered no resistance and flung her arms about his neck and kept her lips fastened to his. He rammed into her and she forced herself to gasp with feigned delight, her eyes carefully watching the open doorway behind his heaving back.

He rutted wildly, grunting with pleasure, his huge erection slamming deep into her with a frantic wildness that meant he was far ahead of her and would soon climax. This mattered little to her, however, and when he began to squeal, she leaned back, waiting for Nate to climax. When he did, he buried his face in her breasts. Reaching up, she stroked his damp hair, her eyes on the open doorway.

Listening intently, she thought she could hear Pete

snoring. She closed her eyes in frustration and then took Nate's face in her hands, lifted him to hers and kissed him on the lips. He returned her kiss hungrily, and she felt him coming to life against her thigh. Reaching down, she felt of him and sighed.

"You are all man, Nate," she said breathlessly, her eyes wide with passion as she gazed into his. "I like you, I think. Very much."

His lips covered her face. "Jesus, Consuela. I like you, too!"

"That is nice," she sighed, her hand stroking his quiescent organ back to life. "Please. Show Consuela again how much you like her."

He responded quickly, feverishly, clambering up onto her like an eager, oversized puppy, thrusting joyously, intent only on his own pleasure. His thighs were slapping loudly on hers now and the bed was squeaking wildly. She began to move rapidly herself and was rewarded by the sound of the bedposts slapping rhythmically against the wall in a beat that grew louder and more rapid with each passing second.

Gazing past Nate's left shoulder she saw Pete step into the bedroom doorway, his hair awry, his sleep-swollen face purpling with fury. He had his sixgun in his hand. As he strode into the bedroom, he raised it.

She screamed, "Nate!"

Nate came alive to the danger instantly. Rolling off her, he snatched his sixgun from his holster. As Consuela threw herself off the bed—landing between it and the wall—two thunderous detonations filled the room. She heard a muffled cry and peered over the edge of the mattress.

Pete was leaning back against the wall, his face pale

with shock. There was a hole in his stomach just above his belly button from which a small ribbon of blood trailed. On the wall behind him there was a growing stain of blood and tissue. Sinking slowly down the wall, Pete brought up his sixgun and managed to squeeze off a second shot at Nate.

But the bullet missed Nate, who was standing by the bed, unscathed, his own smoking Colt in his hand. The fear on his face turned to unabashed triumph when he saw Pete hit the floor, then pitch forward, revealing the gaping hole in his back.

Consuela thought she was going to be sick. She clapped her hand over her mouth, darted from the room, and ran outside. When she came back in a moment later, her stomach still queasy, she saw Nate dragging Pete Kroner's dead body out of his bedroom.

"Hold the kitchen door open for me, will you?" he called to her over his shoulder.

She did as he bid, looking away as Pete's dead body was dragged past her and out into the night.

It was late the next day. Since the night before, Consuela had kept her distance from Nate Heller, as if what had happened had been totally unexpected and had left her shaken. At noon she had taken Pete's rifle and found herself a spot below the cabin, high in some rocks that gave her an unobstructed view of the pass. Just below her was a field strewn with massive boulders that extended a couple of hundred yards down the slope before the timber swallowed it.

She expected Jed Morgan to show before long. He was that kind of man. Tenacious. She hated him for the way he had slung her over his shoulder and dumped her on Bat's bed when she had been so all-fired eager to seduce him. She hated him, but at the same time she respected him. It was unusual to find a man that sure of himself, that unmindful of her charms. She had taken so many men in her life, she regarded them all as slobbering fools with their brains down between their legs.

This Jed Morgan was different. It was a pity she would have to kill him. . . .

"What'n hell you doin' way down here?"

Consuela turned. Nate was climbing up the slight incline to her spot.

"I'm keeping a lookout," she told him, glancing back down at the pass. "We may have visitors before long."

He pulled up beside her and peered past her at the pass below. "Visitors? You got to be kiddin'."

"I mean that fellow I told Pete about, the one calls himself Jed Morgan. He don't quit easy, looks like."

"Hell, we lost him back at the village."

"I think he's still on our trail."

"You sure of that, are you?"

"Sure enough," she replied.

He looked at her for a long moment. "Boy, you *are* a cool one. I thought you'd gone off to pull yourself together 'cause of what happened last night. Instead, here you are mounting guard."

"What happen cannot be helped. It is over now."

"Yeah," he muttered uneasily. "It sure is over—for Pete Kroner." He shook his head. "I never thought he'd go down that easy."

"You must not think about it."

"Hell, why not?" he crowed. "It was you gave me the sand to take him on. You and me, Consuela, we're going to live high off the hog from now on. You won't regret throwin' in with me."

140

She looked full at him for the first time since the night before. Then she smiled. "I know I won't," she said. "You are a very brave man, Nate."

He reached out and grabbed her clumsily. "And right now a very horny one."

Firmly, but as gently as she could, she resisted his advances. The rifle helped. It got between her and him, a cold, unyielding barrier. Nate stepped back, uncertain.

"What's wrong, Consuela? You was sure as hell eager enough last night."

"That was last night. A lot happened since that time."

He straightened himself. "Yeah, sure. Well, it's gettin' time for supper, don't you think?"

She sighed. "I'll be up soon. But maybe you'd better stay down here. Keep watch on the pass."

"Hell, this guy Morgan'll never find us now."

She came suddenly alert. "You don't think so?"

"No."

"Then look down there." She pointed.

At sight of the two riders moving steadily across the parkland toward them, Nate uttered a dismal cry. "Shit!"

"One of them is Morgan," she told him. "The tall one."

"Who's the one with him?"

"I don't know."

Nate took out his sixgun nervously and examined his load. Watching him, she said, "Nate, we got any more of that dynamite?"

"Sure. We still got plenty."

"Good. I have plan."

"Hell, we don't need no plan. We'll wait up here and see if they cut our trail. If they do, we'll be waitin'. It'll be like shooting fish in a barrel."

"This man is not easy to take, I tell you."

"What do you mean? He puts his pants on one leg at a time, just like the rest of us."

"No. He is not like the rest of you."

"What the hell d'you mean by that?" he demanded, bridling.

She was fast losing patience with him, but she ignored his hurt pride and insisted, "I tell you, Nate. We need a plan."

"All right," he said grudgingly, peering anxiously past her through the pines. "But there's still a good chance they'll ride on through the pass and we'll never see them again."

"Yes," she admitted, watching the approaching riders. "That is true."

But she was praying softly that this would not happen—that as Morgan rode across the gravel bed, he would cut their sign. Surely he would be alert enough to catch the telltale scratches and nicks left in the smooth stones by the iron shoes of their struggling pack horses. More than once their horses had plunged their sharp hooves down through the loose gravel and sand as they struggled through it. Pete had been too stupid to notice the sign they were leaving, but she had noticed and was counting heavily on it now.

Her heart leaped. Morgan had pulled up and was looking down at the gravel bed.

"You stay here!" she told Nate, handing him her rifle. "I'm going back up to the cabin. Where's the dynamite?"

"In the barn, alongside the gold."

"I'll get your horse and be right back," she promised him.

"My horse?"

"Sure! You're gonna ride down to them. If they are from the law, they will not draw on you. Tell them how glad you are to see them. Then invite them up. And when they do not suspect a thing, I will blast them out of their saddles."

Nate could hardly believe his ears, but when he looked into Consuela's eyes, he saw a cold, iron resolve that left no doubt in his mind that she was easily capable of doing what she had just said she would do. And in that instant, too, Nate realized just how much of last night's deadly business had been bad luck on Pete's part, and how much had been pure design on Consuela's.

"What's the matter?" she snapped. "Ain't you up to it?"

A feeling of dread fell over him at her cruel taunt. But he did not see how he could argue with her. It was too late for that now. Before he could say anything in response, Consuela had turned and started determinedly back up the slope, heading for the barn.

Nate moistened suddenly dry lips and looked back down at the two horsemen.

Longarm had dismounted and was studying the gravel. Glancing up at Rutger, he pointed to a hole in the gravel and at more telltale disturbances in the gravel bed leading up toward the pines.

"They changed direction here," he said.

Rutger dismounted and hunkered down beside Longarm. "Yep," he said, "clear as mustard on a shirtfront—almost like they're leavin' sign for us to follow."

Longarm stood and peered up through the pines.

"That's just what I was thinking. We better take it careful and figure they're up there waiting. We got two men and a woman to tackle. Bat's one of the men, I'm figuring, 'less he got blown up with the rest. I don't know who the other jasper with him is, but we might as well figure he can fire a gun, too."

"What about the woman?"

"Consuela?" He pondered a moment. "She could sure as hell be trouble, too."

They swung into their saddles and rode up into the pines. In no time they found the game trail, the hoofmarks of the pack horses and saddle horses imprinted firmly in the soft ground wherever the pine needles left a clear spot. They broke out onto a large park littered with huge boulders and pulled up. Peering up the slope past the boulders at the ridge above it, they caught sight of a cabin partially hidden by the pines.

"Hey!"

Turning their heads, both men saw a rider moving out behind one of the boulders, his hand raised in greeting.

"Howdy, strangers!" the fellow called.

Longarm's hand had reached across his belt for his .44 the instant the rider had materialized, and Rutger had already pulled his rifle out of its sling.

"No need for gunplay!" the rider called, pulling up hastily. "I'm not armed."

Longarm looked at Rutger and nodded. Both men put away their weapons. "Come ahead then," Longarm called.

Smiling, the rider rode closer.

"I don't like this," said Longarm.

"Me, neither," Rutger replied.

The rider pulled up in front of them a moment later and shucked his hat back off his forehead. He was still smiling gamely. "I saw you comin' from my cabin up there." He indicated a cabin and some outbuildings on a ridge behind him. "And I thought maybe you'd like some hot coffee and a chance to get off them hurricane decks for a while."

"Real nice of you," said Longarm. He appraised the man coolly, then said, "You wouldn't happen to have any gold lying around, would you?"

The rider shrugged uneasily, his smile fading. "Well now, I guess there's no sense in me trying to deny it."

"The gold's up there?" asked Rutger, surprised they were wrapping this one up so easily.

"It's there, all right," the rider agreed readily. "And it's a curse. Like trying to lug around one of them Egyptian pyramids. Our horses gave out on us."

"Does that mean you're willing to deal?" Rutger asked.

"That's what I'm here for."

"What's your name?" Longarm asked.

"Nate Heller."

"And what's the deal?"

"I take you to the gold, you let me go free."

Longarm looked past Nate up at the cabin. "It's up there, is it?"

"In one of the barns."

"All right. It's a deal. You take us to the gold and we'll give you two days' start. But I want Bat Coulter and Consuela or there's no deal."

"Bat Coulter?"

"You heard me. And Consuela."

"Bat Coulter's dead. Pete Kroner killed him the same

145

day Bat rode into that chink town."

"Why?"

"Hell, Pete didn't have no place for him. Besides, Bat thought *he* was in charge. Pete didn't go for that."

Longarm frowned. Evidently Pete Kroner was the leader of the gang which had taken root in the Celestial City's saloon. Before Longarm and Tom Shan made their move on it, Kroner had already killed Bat and taken the gold for himself.

"Then I want Kroner and Consuela," he told Nate Heller.

What passed for a smirk crossed Heller's face. "It's just me and Consuela now, mister."

Longarm frowned. This gent had somehow managed to dispose of Pete Kroner and was now the sole possessor of all that gold, plus Consuela—and yet he was willing to turn both over in exchange for only two days' start.

Like hell he was!

"You're a liar, Heller!" Longarm said, drawing his Colt. "Now what in hell are you trying to pull?"

Staring into the bore of Longarm's .44, Heller pulled his horse back, then glanced nervously about as if he was looking for—no, *expecting*—someone to bail him out. In that instant Longarm realized what Heller was up to. He was the Judas goat supposed to lead them to Consuela's bushwhacking party.

Before Longarm could warn Rutger, he saw Consuela step out onto a ledge above them, lift a rifle to her shoulder, and fire. The bullet smashed into the rear haunch of Nate Heller's horse. Groaning, it sagged under Heller. Heller flung his head about to stare up at Consuela in pure astonishment. Longarm and Rutger

146

pulled their horses around and were spurring them out of range when Consuela's second round hit the saddle-bag behind Nate Heller's saddle.

The explosion was blinding. A hot fist struck Longarm in the small of the back, punching him off his horse. Unable to get his breath, deafened by the blast, he was trapped in an airless universe of fire and dust as he was sucked high into the air, then slammed brutally back down. His horse came down hard upon him, its bloody heft nearly burying him. He tried to pull himself out from under it, but he could not move a muscle. All the wires were down. He lost consciousness.

How much time passed before he came to, he did not know. It could not have been long. He could hear clearly now and what had awakened him was the sharp click of iron on stone. He opened his eyes. Blood from the dead horse had flowed freely over his face and neck. Through a red haze of bloodied lids, he saw Consuela approaching astride a big chestnut. She pulled up close to him and peered down. From the pinched but deter-mined look on her face, he could see how the sight of all this mangled flesh was affecting her. The moment she caught sight of Longarm's face, she clapped her hand over her mouth, pulled her mount around, and rode off. Leaning back under the horse's dead weight, Longarm heard the clash of shod hooves on the stony slope fade swiftly.

His ears still rang some, but he felt no pain. He was filled with a grim astonishment at how simply and beau-tifully Consuela had contrived to get rid of them. She must have put at least three sticks of dynamite in Nate Heller's saddlebag and he found himself thinking almost sympathetically of that poor, unsuspecting son of a bitch. With a woman like that Nate Heller never had a chance.

And neither, it seemed, had Longarm or Rutger.

Chapter 9

Sometime during the night, Longarm heard horses moving off from the ridge above. He listened carefully, his eyes on the stars—the north star in particular. Consuela was heading south, not west.

By morning he was no longer free of pain. What he felt was a generalized ache that covered his entire body. He remembered having felt the same way once after falling down a flight of steps. He was encouraged by the fact that as he struggled to free himself, he felt no sudden sharp dagger of pain which would have indicated a break. And he did not appear to be losing blood.

He called out to Bob Rutger for a while but got no response, and gave it up to save energy as he increased his efforts to pull himself out from under the horse's dead weight. Eventually he managed to get one arm free, but that was all. His body was wedged in tightly under the lip of a boulder, the horse's haunches pressing down upon him from above with a steadily increasing weight as it settled. He kept on struggling but to no avail, and a slight feeling of panic took hold. He tried to keep it back, despite the cold sweat that had broken out upon his forehead. But by this time he had lost all feeling from the waist down, and it was beginning to dawn on him that if he didn't manage to free himself reasonably soon, he would die where he was, crushed to death under the hindquarters of a dead horse.

He took a deep breath and called out to Rutger a second time. Perhaps the man had only been knocked unconscious earlier and was awake now, sprawled somewhere nearby, wounded. But there was no response. Longarm gave up calling and leaned back to stare up at that portion of the blue sky he was able to glimpse from his prison. Across it swept suddenly the gliding, cinder-like speck of a buzzard. Longarm kept his eye on the blue and saw the buzzard coasting into view again, but lower now, and no longer alone.

Longarm redoubled his efforts. This time he managed to get his other arm free. But this only meant he was now able to reach up with both hands and push desperately against the horse's cold carcass. He might as well have been trying to move a block of granite.

"What happened here?"

Longarm heard the voice, recognized it, but could hardly believe it. Tom Shan was somewhere above him.

"That you, Tom Shan?" he cried.

The sound of a horse's hooves moving closer was followed by the image of Tom Shan astride a big blue, the wide brim of his black Stetson blocking out the patch of blue sky. As he peered down at Longarm, he allowed himself a very slight smile. "Is this the Honorable Knight of the Highway?"

"Get me out of here!"

Tom Shan's smile vanished as he realized more fully Longarm's desperate plight. Dismounting, he dropped a rope around one of the horse's rear legs, mounted back up, then dragged the horse off Longarm, after which he dismounted once again and helped Longarm out from his grisly prison. At once Longarm tried to stand, but he found it impossible.

"My legs," he explained to Tom Shan as he slumped back onto the ground and began rubbing them furiously. "I've lost all feeling in them. The circulation's been stopped for hours."

Hunkering down beside him, Tom Shan indicated the carnage all around with a sweep of his hand. "I still want to know what happened here."

"What does it look like?"

"An explosion. More dynamite?"

Longarm nodded. There was the beginning of a fierce, painful tingling in his right leg that was working its way down to his ankle. He began to rub his left leg.

"Bat Coulter did it?"

"No. Bat Coulter is dead. It was the woman."

"Consuela?"

"Yes."

"How did she manage it?"

"Near as I can figure, she placed dynamite in her accomplice's saddlebag, then detonated it with rifle fire. The poor son of a bitch went up with the rest of us. Have you found Bob Rutger yet?"

"He's on the other side of that boulder where I found

151

you. His head's split open like a melon. He couldn't have felt a thing."

"And the other one?"

"There's pieces of him—and his horse—around here." Tom Shan's slanted eyes went cold as he glanced about him. "All over, as a matter of fact."

By this time the pins-and-needles sensation was running riot in both of Longarm's legs. He leaned back against the face of a boulder and gritted his teeth.

"And where now is this very remarkable woman?" Tom Shan asked. "This humble servant of his ancestors would like very much to meet a woman of such character."

"South. I heard her ride off to the south."

"Why south?"

"How the hell do I know? But south of here's a town called Black Rock. It has just what a fleeing woman with too heavy a load of gold will need. Fresh mounts, clothes, provisions. I figure she will have to show up there sooner or later."

"Then I propose we head for Black Rock."

"What is this, Tom Shan? I would have thought you'd be halfway to San Francisco by now."

"I am no longer the servant of the Ong Leong. I have been in this country of yours since I was ten years old. It is my country now. The land of my ancestors belongs to my ancestors, and it has occurred to me that a man with yellow skin can find a home in such a big country if only he has enough gold to quiet disapproving tongues and buy off all the fools who would force me to leave. So you see, with enough gold, I may remain here as a citizen like any other."

"You don't need gold for that."

"You are a naive man if you believe that."

"Well, I believe it."

"Nevertheless, I will follow the woman Consuela with you—and see what develops. After all, she has a fortune in gold. What does it matter if a few gold bars fall my way?"

"None of it belongs to you, Tom Shan."

"Do not call me Tom Shan. I have a new name now."

"Oh?"

"There is a street in San Francisco where my grandmother brought me up before she gave me over to the keeping of the Ong Leong. It is called Maple Street. Call me Tom Maple."

"It won't make you look any less Chinese."

"But it will assure my escape from the Ong Leong. Chou Li-Fan has put the name of Tom Shan on a gravestone alongside those of my two companions. But there is always the chance the elders will not believe all three of us died assaulting that saloon."

Longarm shrugged. "Tom Maple it is, then."

Longarm's legs felt much stronger now. Pushing himself erect, he looked around and was able to see more of the bloody devastation wrought by the dynamite blast. It sickened him.

The lingering weakness in his legs caused him to move awkwardly for a long while after Tom Maple pulled him free. Nevertheless, they were able to bury Bob Rutger on a small grassy sward overlooking the pine slope. Afterward, standing over the low mound of fresh dark soil that covered Rutger's remains, Longarm doffed his hat and found words difficult. He had grown to like the lanky, taciturn man. Rutger had been a good and faithful deputy. Not once had he flinched from danger, and he had said little on the whole, content to chew on his tobacco. Longarm would miss him. That the man had died in such a sudden, inexplicable way saddened him greatly—and reminded Longarm of the futility of most men's endeavors.

He mumbled the Lord's prayer softly, his head bowed. Then he put his hat back on and straightened up.

"I need a horse," he told Tom Maple.

"Perhaps there's one up there," Tom said, pointing to the cabin and barns visible through the pines above them.

They pulled Longarm's saddle off his dead horse. The rifle was still in its sling. Its stock was scratched, but the firing chamber and pin were in good condition and the barrel had not been bent when the horse came down. Mounting up behind Tom Maple, they rode on up the slope to the cabin and found two horses—a gray and a worn-out mare—in one of the barns. Both of them were weak for want of water and grain. They brought the animals water and grain and the next morning they set out for Black Rock, Longarm riding the gray and setting the mare free.

There was no more talk from Tom Maple about the gold he was counting on taking from Consuela, so Longarm put that item out of his mind for now. His hope was that when the time came, he and Tom would be able to work something out.

At least, he hoped so. After all, Tom Maple had just saved his life.

Consuela sat back on the rock and mopped her brow, the shovel still in her hand. The sun was mean and hot and

154

unwavering and she peered up at it through narrowed eyes, as if she were daring it to do its worst. Having no more need of the shovel she had taken from the cabin, she flung it away, then pulled the Stetson's brim down to shield her eyes. The Stetson had belonged to Pete Kroner and was a size too big for her, but she had stuffed a strip torn from her skirt inside the brim and it now fit her reasonably enough.

She should have been discouraged, but she wasn't. She had expected to lose most or all of the pack horses by this time and she was reasonably certain that her map, no matter how crude it was, would be sufficiently helpful to enable her to retrieve the gold she had been burying for the past two days.

She took out the map and smoothed it down onto a flat rock. Carefully wetting the end of her pencil, she drew a line representing the trail she had taken to this huge boulder and then a crude representation of it, placing an X close under it. Folding the map, she placed it back in her blouse, and move back down the narrow game trail. Glancing back at the large, bearlike rock she had selected for a marker, she thought a moment; then, using a soft rock as a piece of chalk, she scratched a crude arrow on the side of a boulder alongside the trail.

Lugging the gold-laden aparejos up the narrow game trail to the great boulder had been exhausting business and had taken her almost the entire morning. The last of the pack horses she had let loose the night before. But even though she knew there was no likelihood of her being followed, she was too anxious about the gold to hang back now.

She mounted the black she had saved for this moment and gently urged the powerful mount on down the

155

trail, still heading south for Black Rock. Her horse was as fresh as it would ever be, and Consuela had no doubt it would be strong enough to carry the many sacks of gold dust she had crowded into her two saddlebags. Black Rock was only a few miles farther on. She knew the place well enough. It was where she had met Bat Coulter. Once there, she would find some other fool to seduce. When the time was ripe, she would purchase as many wagons as would be needed to collect the gold she had buried, and when it was all retrieved, she would dispose of her male partner just as easily as she had the others.

It was strange—and also just a bit exhilarating—to realize how simple it was for her to rid herself of men. She used to let men bully and use her. Still, she told herself not to dwell unduly on this, and urged her horse on through the midday heat.

She rode into Black Rock a day later at high noon, wearing her hair in a long braid down her back, her long limbs astride the big black like a man, wearing a man's pants, shirt, and vest and a Stetson a size too large for her. Its wide brim cast her upper face in shadow, so that at first only her bold chin was visible to onlookers. She rode slowly, giving every man in the town a good long look at her before she nudged the black into the livery stable.

Not long after, the waiting townsmen got a glimpse of her moving across the street to the two-story hotel, a rifle in one hand and a gunbelt snugged about her narrow waist, her dark eyes flashing imperiously as she gazed neither to the right nor the left. Behind her came Lafe Warren, the stableboy. He was staggering under the load of two saddlebags. Not a man lounging on the hotel porch or in front of the two saloons across the street missed the significance of Lafe's struggle with those two saddlebags. Especially when word got out almost immediately afterward that the woman paid the desk clerk for her room in advance with pure, unadulterated gold dust she took from a small leather pouch hung about her neck.

Not long after, Consuela left the hotel for a bit of shopping, visiting the small town's three shops, leaving each after several purchases. The things were delivered back to her hotel room. She appeared on the hotel porch a little before nightfall, dressed in finery that any woman of Paris might envy. Her dark, striking beauty added a dimension to the elegant, silken folds of her long, bottle-green skirt and jacket that turned every head.

She waited imperiously for a seat at one of the three tables set out on the porch. It was provided for her almost immediately as a portly gentleman in a checked vest hastily vacated it, indicating with a slight bow that she was welcome to it. She thanked him with the slightest breath of a smile, swept over to it, and sat down.

At once a waiter brought her coffee and some small cakes on a small silver platter.

Consuela knew what she was doing. She was advertising. It would not be long before some fool would decide to pluck this gold-laden female. He would tighten his string tie, square his shoulders, mount the porch, and make an approach. Patiently she waited, sipping her coffee, reminding herself that she would have to be careful that the fool she chose was not *too* much of fool.

She had taken a flask from her handbag and was adding a little backbone to her coffee when heavy bootheels sounded on the porch. She glanced up and saw approaching her a tall, raw-boned fellow with long, dark hair and an eager glint in his hazel eyes. *Here he comes,* she hoped—not yet sure she liked the cut of him, but certain she could handle him.

"Howdy, ma'am," he said, removing his hat. "Mind if I join you?"

She indicated with a glance the empty chair beside her. "It's a free country."

"It is that," he breathed happily, slumping quickly down into the chair and dropping his hat by his chair. "Yes, it is."

Sipping her coffee, she looked at him over the rim. This closer inspection disappointed her. She recognized in his face a tell-tale vacancy which betrayed a man not overly endowed with intelligence, no matter how broad his shoulders or how long his reach.

"Nice night, ain't it," the gentleman said.

"Yes."

"My name's Buck Kincaid," he said, smiling, and Consuela noticed that he had excellent teeth. Indeed, it *was* like picking a horse, after all, she reminded herself.

"My name's Consuela."

He waited for the rest of her name, but Consuela said nothing more. She picked up her coffee, sipped it, and gazed somewhat impatiently out over the porch railing at the many townspeople passing the hotel. It seemed to her that the traffic had increased considerably since she stepped out onto the porch.

She waited for Buck Kincaid to bring up the weather again, but he was too busy preening himself. Leaning back in his chair, he gazed proudly out over the passing parade. The new girl in town had let him join her, and

158

his triumph was on display for all to see and admire.

Consuela decided she might as well accept what chance had brought her. Not especially happy at the prospect, she steeled herself into inviting Buck Kincaid to her room for the night. She did not think this would be very difficult.

She pulled her dark shawl up around her neck. "I do believe it is getting chilly," she said.

"Sun's going down," he replied, exhibiting remarkable insight.

"It does get *so* chilly in these mountains at night."

"Yes, it does, ma'am."

"I'll have to go back to my room to get something warmer," she confided, her eyes catching his. She smiled then, meltingly. "Would you care to accompany me?"

"To—to your room?"

"Yes," she replied, suddenly furious, sure now that this swell did not have the stuff she would need.

"I'll—I'll wait right here," the fool replied hastily.

"Then wait," she said testily. "I'll be retiring for the night."

She got up then, unable to quell her disappointment.

Another heavy pair of boots struck the porch and headed toward her. Consuela glanced over to see a man of a very different stripe approaching. At once she quickened. This was more like it.

The newcomer was not as tall as Buck Kincaid, and he was somewhat blockier in build, but there was a reckless gleam in his eye and she knew at once that this man knew women. His hair and trim mustache were blond. As he looked her over, his teeth flashed in a quick, appreciative grin.

"Leaving, ma'am?" he said.

159

"I was thinking of going upstairs for something warmer."

"It is getting chilly, isn't it. What say you do that. Then we'll make the rounds. Are you a gambling woman, by any chance?"

She met his smile with one of her own. "I am," she acknowledged. "I'll be right down, Mr.—?"

"Swenson. Carl Swenson."

"I am Consuela."

"I'll be waiting right here, Consuela," Swenson replied, doffing his hat gallantly.

Behind him Buck Kincaid was slinking off the porch, anxious not to offend Carl Swenson, it appeared. Good. She had finally met the head buck. She turned and entered the hotel.

Everything was going to be fine. Just fine.

Just a little weary from the smoke and the noise and still hearing faintly the clink of chips, she stood by the door while Carl lit the lamp by her bed and then the lamp on the dresser. It had been a long day for her. All she hoped now was that she was up to what lay ahead. She had her man in her parlor. Now she had to weave her web about him.

He turned to face her. She smiled, took off her jacket, and flung it over a chair. Then she began to unbutton her blouse. She did it slowly, savoring each button's release, while she watched him.

"You don't waste much time," he said, "do you?"

"It has been a long day for me."

"If you want, I'll come back tomorrow."

"You bastard," she said, smiling softly at him. "You know you can't do that to me—or to you."

He walked over to the bed, sat on its edge, and

pulled off his boots. "I reckon that's the pure truth of it, Consuela. How much did you win?"

"A few hundred," she replied, unsnapping her skirt.

"Never saw a woman play so recklessly."

"When you don't care if you lose, that's how you play." She stepped out of her skirt and flung it over the back of a chair by the window.

"You purchased your chips with gold dust."

"Yes."

"The word in town is that you also paid for this room with gold dust."

Peeling off her silk petticoat, she glanced at him. "Is there anything wrong with that?"

He was sitting on the bed, still with his pants on, looking closely at her.

"What's the matter?" she asked him. "Ain't you up to it?"

He frowned, not liking the remark, but said nothing and began peeling off his pants. Dressed only in her chemise, she moved over to the window and looked down. Newly installed gaslights cast a pale, yellowish glow over the street.

She wanted him to come over to the window and make the first move. Why this was so important to her she did not know. But she wanted it. For hours she had been throwing out all the hints, making all the promises, with word and gesture. Now she wanted him to invest something in this endeavor as well.

Stark naked, he walked over to her and put both arms around her waist. She could feel his rigid member nudging the small of her back. It was as if a flame had broken loose inside her. She turned to him and they kissed passionately.

When they broke, he looked down at her and

grinned. "Been wanting to do that all night."

"Me, too," she told him, throwing aside her chemise. Taking his hand, she led him over to the bed.

Later, bathed in the warm afterglow of their passionate coupling, Consuela told Carl everything she wanted him to know and not one bit more. Without explaining how she had managed it, she told him she had taken gold from a gang that had recently robbed a train. On the way to Black Rock, she had hidden the gold. But she had a map and in a few weeks, when the heat from the train robbery had faded, she planned to purchase wagons and, using her map, retrieve all the gold. All she wanted from Carl was his promise to help her. If he would do so, she promised to share the gold with him equally.

He knew at once which train robbery she was referring to and seemed astounded at her words, but there was no doubt he believed her. Her possession of the gold dust made everything she said fall into place. There was no doubt also that he was hooked.

This was his lucky day, and he knew it.

The only thing that bothered Consuela was the part of the plan she had not revealed to Carl Swenson, the part where she got rid of him as she had the others. She hoped grimly that when the time came she would be able to get the thing done without messing it up.

He had been watching her intently for a moment. "Why the frown?"

"No reason," she said.

He reached out and pulled her around so that she could not evade looking deep into his eyes. "You aren't planning anything untidy, are you?"

162

"Of course not."

"That's good. This is a partnership, Consuela. And a partnership is as hard to break up as a marriage."

"You don't need to worry."

"And neither do you. I'll hold up my end of the bargain."

"That's all I want, Carl."

"Fine."

He pulled her closer and kissed her warmly. She felt a tremor. This man had a way with her. He seemed to be able to cut close to where she lived. This had never happened to her before. She had never let it.

Restless, she got up, went to the window, and looked down. The room was dark. She had no difficulty seeing the street. It was practically deserted now, the streetlamps sending a soft light over the closed shops and empty sidewalks.

She heard the sound of horses' hooves and waited. Two riders came into her line of sight. She gasped softly. A man she herself had blown to Kingdom Come was riding into town, and beside him an Oriental she had never seen before. Reaching out, she took hold of the curtains and almost pulled them down.

Carl was beside her in an instant. "What is it?"

"Those two men down there. They—they're after me."

"You mean they're after the gold?"

"Yes."

"Who are they?"

"One of them, the Chinese, I've never seen before. The other is a man called Morgan, Jed Morgan. I think he's a lawman."

"You look like you've seen a ghost."

She nodded numbly. "I thought Morgan was dead."

"You mean you tried to kill him."

"Yes."

"Looks like you do need me after all."

"What—what are you going to do?"

"Finish what you started."

"How?"

Carl watched the two men dismount in front of the livery. "I'll invite them up here. It's you they're after, ain't it?"

"But if there's gunplay, we'll be caught."

"If it comes to that, I can handle the town marshal. Him and me are good poker buddies. If he won't go along, we might have to share some of the gold with him, but don't worry. It won't come to that because there'll be no gunplay. A knock on the head is as good as a bullet, and I'll get them up here before anyone even knows they're in town." He turned from the window. "Think you can handle your part in this?"

She was feeling better already. It was amazing how much like her Swenson was. Bringing Morgan and the other one up here was the ideal solution. "Yes," she said, "I'm up to it. I'll have them covered as soon as they enter the room, and you'll have them covered from behind."

He smiled, pleased at her composure.

"But suppose they won't come up here with you?" she went on.

"I know how much gold was taken from that train, Consuela. That's a powerful incentive—not only for me, but for those two gents downstairs. Don't worry. They'll come up."

• • •

164

Longarm tossed the hostler a coin and stepped out of the stable with Tom. The hotel across the street looked shut down, except for the lobby downstairs, where a dim light glowed. At that moment the prospect of a bed off the ground and the feel of clean sheets was very inviting. They walked across the street and mounted the porch steps.

A dark figure sitting in a chair at the far end of the porch cleared his throat. Longarm halted and glanced over at him. Tom pulled up also. The stranger got to his feet. His Colt's long barrel gleamed in the streetlamps' pale light.

"Stay nice and quiet, gents," the fellow said, moving swiftly toward them.

The stranger with the Colt was of a blocky build, with blond hair and mustache, and eyes cold and efficient. Disarming Tom, he found Longarm's revolver after a quick pat on Longarm's left side. But he did not give the watch chain looping across Longarm's vest to his derringer a second look. Waggling his Colt's barrel at them, he indicated that they should proceed into the hotel ahead of him.

Longarm did not budge. "Just who in the hell are you, mister, and what're you up to?" he demanded

The fellow chuckled. "Consuela's been expecting you gents," he said. "If you want to get your hands on the gold she's hid, get inside."

Longarm glanced at Tom. Tom shrugged. With a weary sigh, Longarm entered the hotel. The desk clerk was nowhere in sight. With Tom moving ahead of him, Longarm started up the stairs. Every now and then, just to keep Longarm honest, the gent behind him would thrust the muzzle of his sixgun into the small of the

165

lawman's back. Longarm was furious for allowing himself to be taken this easily. How many times, he wondered, was he going to be bushwhacked by Consuela? If he wasn't careful, one of these times she was going to succeed.

On the second floor they proceeded down a hallway to a door slightly ajar. Lamplight flooded out from under it.

"Go on," said their captor, "get inside."

Tom pushed the door open and entered, Longarm following on his heels. Consuela stood in front of the bed in a white robe with a revolver in her hand. She smiled coldly and Longarm thought he saw her trigger finger tightening. He shoved Tom violently aside and dove to the floor. Startled, Consuela jumped back, the gun in her hand detonating. At the same time a shot came from her partner. Consuela clutched at her waist and crumpled to the floor, blood oozing between her fingers, turning her robe to crimson.

Fumbling for his derringer, Longarm rolled over and brought it up in time to empty both barrels into the blond gent's chest. The man toppled forward into the room, dead before he hit the floor.

Longarm got to his feet and walked over to the dead man, then glanced at the doorjamb and saw where Consuela's bullet had lodged in it. He glanced back at Consuela. Still clutching at her wound, she was writhing slowly on the floor. Tom and Longarm knelt by her. She was gutshot and would not last long, the men realized.

She opened her eyes and stared up at him in disbelief. "You . . . !" she cried softly. "Who are you? A lawman?"

"Yes, Consuela."

"Damn you!"

"Where's the gold?" he asked her.

". . . Hid it. You'll . . . never find it," she gasped defiantly.

Behind them in the open door, a crowd of men and women was gathering. Longarm turned and told one of them to go for the doctor and the town marshal. Two men dressed in robes broke back down the hallway.

Longarm looked back at Consuela. "Consuela, I want Les. You got any idea where he went?"

She grinned tightly, still gasping in pain. In a thin voice she said, "He . . . smart one. Went back to . . . wife."

Longarm nodded and stood up. When he and Rutger had watched Les riding out from Celestial City, he had guessed right. As the doctor pushed into the room, the town marshal right behind him, Longarm pulled the marshal to one side.

Without his badge, he had some explaining to do.

The sheriff in Red Cliff was surprised to see Longarm. With some difficulty, he pushed his bulk upright and crossed the room. Longarm tossed two heavy saddlebags over the arm of a wooden chair and the two men shook hands.

"Thought you'd disappeared for good," Sheriff Scott told him. "Where's Bob Rutger?"

"He won't be coming back."

Sheriff Scott frowned. "What happened?"

"It's too complicated to go into now, Sheriff. Later, if you don't mind."

"It's just that we all liked Bob. When his pa was killed, that left him alone to run their spread. He

167

worked mighty hard, but we all knew his heart was no longer in it—not with his father gone like that."

"I got a map for you. Found it in one of those saddle-bags, along with the sacks of gold dust in it."

"A map? What do I want with a map?"

"If the owners of the Link Mine want the rest of their gold back, or at least a good deal of it, they'll follow this map. There's places marked on it where the gold was hid. I got someone who can go over the trail with them. The thing is, they'll need wagons for hauling back the gold."

"Someone? What about you?"

"I got other business."

"What's more important than regaining this gold?"

"There's one more member of the gang still at large. I want him. I want him bad."

Sheriff Scott scratched his unshaven face. "I see."

Tom Maple stepped into the sheriff's office. The handsome Oriental nodded to the sheriff as he came to a halt next to Longarm. "This here's Tom Maple, Sheriff. He's the one can help you figure out that map."

The sheriff looked carefully at Tom. "You know the territory, do you?"

"Well enough."

The sheriff shrugged. "Then I guess that'll have to be it."

Tom turned to Longarm. "Before you ride out, there's something I got to tell you, Longarm."

Longarm looked back at the sheriff. "We'll be in the saloon down the street," he told him.

The sheriff nodded and went over to inspect the two saddlebags Longarm had thrown over the chair. Longarm and Tom walked down a block and entered the Red

Cliff Saloon and Gambling Hall. Longarm was pleased to find that they stocked Maryland rye. Tom Maple asked for some plum wine, but got only a stare in response. The two men found a table in the rear and shared Longarm's rye.

"Now, what's this you got to tell me?" Longarm asked Tom.

"I looked at the map. There's one place where there's supposed to be gold—the one near Celestial City."

Longarm sipped the whiskey. "So?"

"There's no gold there."

"How do you know?"

"I already found it."

"You what?"

"That's right. I was trailing them, like you were. They tried to hide their tracks, but they didn't do a very good job of it, and I found the cave where they hid a good portion of the gold."

"Where is it now?"

Tom smiled. "The aged survivors of Celestial City have it. And if I am not mistaken, they are now well on their way to the coast—and from there, to the land of my ancestors. With that much gold, they won't have to deal with the Ong Leong to obtain passage. At least that is what Chou Li-Fan assured me."

Longarm leaned back in his chair and considered this carefully, then shrugged. "Well, then, I guess I'll just have to forget you told me this—if you promise to keep your sticky hands off any of that gold you help the Link Mine recover."

Relieved, Tom nodded. "It's a deal."

Longarm finished his glass, poured himself another, and then refilled Tom's glass. He guessed he was doing the right thing. As Tom Maple insisted—and he was probably right—in years past the owners of the Link Mine, like so many others in the region, had exploited the Chinese fearfully, only to sack them when their coolie labor was no longer profitable.

Those old men and women sent back to the Celestial City by the Ong Leong to dig for jade deserved this one final chance to make it back all the way to the Pearl River delta and to see again the rice fields and the Pagoda of Nine Stories.

Chapter 10

Serena's ranch was suspiciously quiet, Longarm noted as he pulled his mount to a halt on the ridge and looked down the long sweep of the parkland to the distant cluster of ranch buildings. There were no horses that he could see grazing in the distant pasture lapping the mountain's long flank. And there was no smoke coming from the ranch house chimney. He pulled his mount back off the ridge and lost sight of the ranch buildings. A concerned frown on his face, he put his horse back onto the trail that wound down through the thick pine and aspen.

Lester tossed aside the shovel and gazed back for a minute at the fresh mound of dirt that covered Abe's smashed body. He should have felt remorse, he supposed. But he felt nothing—only relief to be rid of the meddling old son of a bitch. What gave that bastard the right to come between a man and his lawful wedded wife? Brushing off his hands, Les started back up the slope to the ranch house, looking forward eagerly to the unfinished business ahead of him. Now it was Serena's turn to feel the lash of his resolve. He felt pretty damn confident. Surely now that she knew what kind of man she was dealing with, her stubborn refusal to go to bed with him would come to an end.

No woman respected a man who didn't knock her around every once in a while to show her who was boss. And he had sure as hell been busy doing that ever since he got back. He had just killed an old meddling fool who had tried to stand in his way. Serena would have to respect his resolve now. There would be no more foolishness.

Watching Lester approach the ranch house, Serena's fierce determination nearly deserted her. Ever since he had left to bury poor Abe's body, she had been waiting for his return, while at the same time praying that he would not return at all. His killing Abe in a blind rage had made him an outlaw, so his best course would be to flee—to ride out and never look back.

But of course Lester did not have that much sense. With Lester things could not be that simple. He was close enough now for her to see the childish resolve on his face—even the mean, eager gleam in his eyes. And she knew what that meant.

Her moment of panic passed and she tightened her grip on the large carving knife she had sharpened especially for this deed. Moving into the shadows beside the doorway, she brought the weapon up over her right shoulder and braced herself to bring it down with sufficient force. Lester's footsteps were clearer now. She could almost smell the man's sweaty, unwashed body. Then the doorway darkened as Lester's bulk filled it.

As he stepped inside, Serena slashed down. But Lester had caught her movement out of the corner of his eye. Just as the blade began its furious, slashing arc, he turned and flung up his right forearm, managing to ward off the blow. Serena felt the blade catch the sleeve of his jacket. The knife's tip got snagged in the cloth and the knife penetrated nothing. Before she could bring it back for another downward thrust, Lester's clenched fist caught her on the point of her jaw.

She sagged back, dazed, and felt him twist her right wrist. She gasped in pain and dropped the knife. With a snarl of pleasure, he plucked up the knife and stuck it in his belt. Then he lifted her in his arms and strode toward the bedroom. At once she realized his intentions. It drove her wild with fury. She began beating upon him as she had done so often before. But this time it did no good. Her blows only seemed to strengthen him, to increase his lust for her.

He flung her down onto the bed. The mattress caught her in the small of the back. She felt her breath explode from her lungs and tried to roll aside, but his dark bulk was too quick for her. Then he was on her, catching at her flailing fists in an effort to pin them down.

While she struggled, he managed to kick off his boots and slip out of his pants, the knife clattering to the floor. Naked from the waist down, he leaned heavily on her, breathing hard, his yellow teeth like a dog's fangs. He was enjoying himself hugely. As they struggled, sweat from his face dropped onto her neck. Each drop chilled her to the bone.

She increased her struggling, reaching up in an attempt to get a fingernail into one of his eyes. Lester grunted as her right hand, frozen into a claw, raked down the right side of his face. He sat back, his legs still straddling her, measured her happily, then brought his right fist around. He had aimed for the tip of her chin, but she managed to swing her face away and the blow caught her high on the left cheekbone. She felt the skin begin to swell almost at once. Insane with fury now, she grabbed his left wrist with both hands and pulled it down to her mouth. Sinking her teeth into the sweaty, grimy flesh nauseated her, but she hung on grimly, aware of Lester's abrupt cry of dismay. She clenched her teeth down even more tightly. Moaning, Lester struck repeatedly at her face with his free hand. This only caused her to tighten her jaws grimly, her eyes closed, hanging on with the tenacity of a bulldog. The salty warmth of his blood filled her mouth and she felt it streaming down her chin as he swiped repeatedly, desperately, at her face.

At last one awful, vicious blow fogged her resolve. She felt her jaws slacken, and then he had pulled his wrist free. Still groggy from his blows to her head, she tried to scramble out from under him. But Lester grabbed the neck of her dress and with a quick, powerful yank ripped it open all the way to her waist. After two more swift yanks, she lay naked before him.

He struck her again in the face to warn her, then mounted her deliberately, the powerful, animal stench of him aroused to a peak by the recent struggle. As he thrust home he cried out in lusty triumph. She felt herself pulling back deep within herself, blacking it all out in a desperate effort to tell herself—and her body—that this was not really happening to her.

In a moment he had exploded deep within her. As

174

she felt his semen pouring into her, she began to cry, the sobs welling up unbidden, racking her beaten, limp body.

Lester rolled off Serena and made no effort to sit up. A delicious drowsiness had fallen over him. He was unmindful of her tears. Hell, she always cried. She just didn't know enough to lay back and enjoy it. Sometimes he thought he'd prefer a bought woman—until he reminded himself that they felt nothing at all, just put on a show for the customer's benefit.

He looked down at his bleeding wrist. He flexed his fingers. It would be all right. He would taunt her with it, later—calling it a love bite.

From outside the ranch house came a soft footfall. Alerted at once, he sat up. The outside door was still wide open, as was the door leading into the bedroom, and Lester could see from the bedroom clear out to the well.

What he saw now astounded him.

It was Longarm, his mouth a cold, hard line as he peered through the open doorway into the ranch house. He had been alerted by Serena's crying, and was holding a Colt in his hand.

Where in hell had the son of a bitch come from? Bat had sent Red Larson after him, and that was the last Lester had heard of either man. Lester had just assumed that both men had taken each other out.

As Longarm stepped from the brightness of the front yard into the gloom of the cabin, Lester snatched up the butcher knife from the floor. Grabbing Serena's hair, he hauled her off the bed and stepped out of the bedroom with her, the knife blade slicing into the white flesh just under Serena's chin.

"Hold it right there, Morgan," Lester said. "One step

175

further, and I'll sink this blade in all the way."

Longarm held up, crouching, peering through the gloom. Coming from the bright outside, he was having difficulty picking out Lester and Serena. Serena tried to twist away. Lester flung his arm about her shoulders and squeezed her back against him, shielding him almost entirely. At the same time, he allowed the knife's sharp point to bite still deeper.

By now, Longarm could see clearly the bright tracery of blood snaking down Serena's neck and across one breast. Serena tried to get away from Lester, but her struggles were futile.

"Stay still, Serena," Longarm told her. "Don't move. He'll kill you."

Lester smiled. "That's talking sense, Morgan. Now drop that Colt."

Longarm dropped the revolver onto the floor.

Lester flung Serena from him and strode quickly forward, his yellow teeth flashing in his face. He kicked Longarm's .44 into a far corner and before Longarm could reach for his derringer, Lester had drawn his own Colt from its holster hanging on the back of a kitchen chair. Thumb-cocking it, he leveled the revolver on Longarm.

"Guess you must've took care of Red Larson, Morgan," Les said, chuckling meanly. "I don't mind. I hated the son of a bitch. I'd pin a medal on you if you'd stand still for it. But I guess you wouldn't."

"No, I wouldn't."

On the floor, her hand up to her bleeding neck, Serena told Longarm, "Lester just killed Abe. He beat him to death."

Longarm looked back at Lester. "That's a hanging offense, Lester."

176

"I know it. And now she's opened her big mouth I'm going to have to kill you."

He lifted the revolver and aimed it. At that instant Serena flung herself up at him, knocking his firing arm to one side. The gun detonated, and Longarm felt the slug tear into his left shoulder, spinning him back out through the open doorway. Sprawled on the low porch, he saw Lester turn on Serena. In a sudden, towering rage, he brought his gun around with vicious force, catching her on the side of the head. As Serena went flying backward, Longarm managed to palm his derringer.

Steadying it on the floor just inside the doorway, he fired up at Lester. The first bullet caught the man in the thigh. He went down on one knee, but spun around doggedly to return Longarm's fire. Before he could, Longarm fired a second time. The .44 calibre slug entered Lester's right eye, exploding the socket inward and pulling the rest of his face in after it. The top of Lester's head dissolved in a bloody corona that splattered the wall behind him. He fell back woodenly, already dead, and slumped over onto the floor.

Longarm poured Billy Vail another drink. It was good whiskey, the Windsor Hotel's finest and Vail's favorite, but it wasn't Maryland rye—and that was a shame, because Longarm felt like celebrating. His left shoulder was almost completely mended now, and Serena had arrived on the four o'clock train.

"...All I'm saying," Vail protested without too much fervor, "is that this Chinese cowboy you gave that map to sure ain't led them mine owners to very much gold."

"But he has led them to some, hasn't he?"

177

"He has."

"Well, then. Tom Maple's doing his best. That's rough country up there. I can testify to that, Billy. Lightning out of a clear blue sky. Towering, snow-capped peaks brushing the clouds. Strange towns built by Orientals. Who knows what else?"

"All right, all right," Vail said wearily. "Spare me the details. Forget I mentioned it. The important thing is you got the Bat Coulter gang. Are you sure you got them all."

"Every one."

Billy Vail looked at him and smiled sardonically. "Including the husband of the woman you escorted from the train station this afternoon." He chuckled at Longarm's surprise. "My spies are everywhere, Longarm."

"So it appears."

"She's upstairs now, ain't she?"

"Ask your spies."

Vail finished his drink. "I won't keep you. Thanks for the drink." He stood up and looked down at his deputy. "You think that shoulder of yours is mended enough? I got a job for you."

"Will it wait?"

"For how long?"

"Give me until next Monday."

"Fair enough."

Vail slapped his hat on and strode off. Longarm dropped some coins to cover the drinks and followed Vail out of the saloon and over to the wide stairs leading to the hotel's second floor. A moment later, Serena answered his light tap on the door. Her hair was combed out and she had put on a long rose-colored dressing gown.

"I'm all unpacked," she said, pulling the door open and stepping aside. "I just couldn't wait to get out of that traveling outfit. It was so tight! I hope you don't mind."

"Why should I mind?" he asked, entering.

Serena closed the door and walked into his arms. He kissed her. She pulled away, smiling.

"When are we going to look at the horses?"

"Tomorrow," he told her. "I've hired a carriage to take us out to the stud farm. If we bring a picnic lunch, it could make for a nice day."

"If it doesn't rain."

He shrugged and took off his jacket, then unbuttoned his vest. She saw what he was doing and smiled approvingly.

"Let's have a picnic up here," she said, eyes glowing. "I've already sent for a waiter."

"Sounds like a fine idea."

There was a light rap on the door. Serena answered it, gave the boy her order, then closed the door and turned to face Longarm. "I told the boy to leave the cart outside the door when he brings it up," she told him. "That way we won't be disturbed."

She walked into his arms and began unbuttoning his shirt. As she peeled it back, she looked at his shoulder wound, a slight frown puckering her brow. "It does look so much better, " she said, pleased. "Does it hurt?"

"Only when I laugh."

"When will you be returning to work?"

"Next Monday."

"That gives us the rest of the week."

"Yes, it does."

As she unbuttoned his pants, she said, "There's only

one thing that still bothers me."

His pants dropped. She leaned against him, her warm hand moving over his chest, then down past his waist, slipping around behind him, pulling him hard against her. He realized then that she was wearing nothing at all under the dressing gown.

"What is it that still bothers you?" He opened her gown and stepped closer.

She gasped as she felt him. "That stolen gold dust Lester brought back with him."

Longarm bent his knees slightly. She walked to him and he felt himself enter her. "He was your husband, wasn't he?"

"Yes," she admitted, shuddering.

"Well, it's yours, then."

"But it was stolen."

"Did you see anything on that gold dust that says Link Mine?" he asked.

"No."

"Did the bank clerk when you deposited it?"

"Of course not."

Longarm stepped closer until he was well inside her. Then he lifted her by the thighs. She tightened them around his waist and locked her ankles. His arms clasped tightly around her back, he carried her over to the bed. His shoulder did not protest in the slightest. Letting her down gently under him, he kissed her eyelids, her nose, then her lips. Her arms snaked about his neck as she drew him down onto her, her legs still scissoring his waist.

"Then I can keep the gold dust?" she said, gasping.

"If you'll just shut up about it and spend it on good horseflesh. Maybe someday you'll be able to pay back the Link Mine with interest."

"You mean, think of it as a loan!"

"Precisely."

She started to say something more, but he closed his mouth over hers and insinuated his tongue gently between her lips. Her mouth opened eagerly, as did her thighs, and he plunged deep inside her.

As he began stroking, she murmured contentedly, and there was no more talk about gold dust. When the knock came on the door indicating their picnic lunch had arrived and was waiting on its cart outside their door, they paid no attention.

Eating would come later. Much later. They were too busy now satisfying other appetites.

Watch for

LONGARM ON THE OVERLAND TRAIL

one hundred and fourth novel in the bold
LONGARM series from Jove

coming in August!

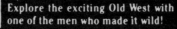